EOIN COLFER'S
ARTEMIS FOWL
THE ETERNITY CODE

Adapted by
EOIN COLFER
&
ANDREW DONKIN

Art by GIOVANNI RIGANO

Colour by PAOLO LAMANNA
Colour Separation by STUDIO BLINQ

Lettering by CHRIS DICKEY

PUFFIN BOOKS

Published by the Penguin Group
Penguin Books Ltd, 80 Strand, London WC2R 0RL, England
Penguin Group (USA) Inc., 375 Hudson Street, New York, New York 10014, USA
Penguin Group (Canada), 90 Eglinton Avenue East, Suite 700, Toronto, Ontario,
Canada M4P 2Y3 (a division of Pearson Penguin Canada Inc.)
Penguin Ireland, 25 St Stephen's Green, Dublin 2, Ireland (a division of Penguin Books Ltd)
Penguin Group (Australia), 707 Collins Street, Melbourne, Victoria 3008, Australia
(a division of Pearson Australia Group Pty Ltd)
Penguin Books India Pvt Ltd, 11 Community Centre, Panchsheel Park,
New Delhi – 110 017, India
Penguin Group (NZ), 67 Apollo Drive, Rosedale, Auckland 0632, New Zealand
(a division of Pearson New Zealand Ltd)
Penguin Books (South Africa) (Pty) Ltd, Block D, Rosebank Office Park, 181 Jan Smuts Avenue,
Parktown North, Gauteng 2193, South Africa

Penguin Books Ltd, Registered Offices: 80 Strand, London WC2R 0RL, England

www.puffinbooks.com

Adapted by Eoin Colfer and Andrew Donkin from the novel *Artemis Fowl and the Eternity Code*,
published in Great Britain by Puffin Books

First published in the USA by Disney • Hyperion Books, an imprint of Disney Book Group, 2013
Published in Great Britain by Puffin Books 2014
001

Text copyright © Eoin Colfer, 2013
Illustrations copyright © Giovanni Rigano, 2013
Colour by Paolo Lamanna
Lettering by Chris Dickey
All rights reserved

The moral right of the author and illustrator has been asserted

Printed in Italy by Graphicom

British Library Cataloguing in Publication Data
A CIP catalogue record for this book is available from the British Library

ISBN: 978–0–141–35026–4

Visit www.artemisfowl.co.uk

www.greenpenguin.co.uk

MIX
Paper from
responsible sources
FSC
www.fsc.org   FSC™ C018179

Penguin Books is committed to a sustainable
future for our business, our readers and our
planet. This book is made from paper certified
by the Forest Stewardship Council.

My name is Artemis Fowl, and I am a genius.

The last two years have been extraordinary, even by my own high standards.

It had all started with the Internet. But then, these days, it always does.

Trawling across the Web, I compiled a database from the millions of references to fairies from all over the world.

There was no doubt the reports referred to the same hidden race.

With the assistance of my faithful bodyguard, Butler, I acquired and then decoded a copy of the fairy race's most secret and hidden text.

Fairies are real.

Several thousand years ago they had moved their whole civilization underground to escape from human eyes.

Their main sanctuary was Haven City, hidden deep beneath the surface of the Earth.

With the help of Butler, I "obtained" one of the fairy creatures...

...an elf named Holly Short, a captain in the elite section of the LEP—Lower Elements Police.

During her brief captivity, there were several frank exchanges of views between Captain Short and myself.

After some rather tense negotiations, Holly left Fowl Manor. She was exchanged with her people for half a ton of fairy gold.

All this before I was thirteen years old.

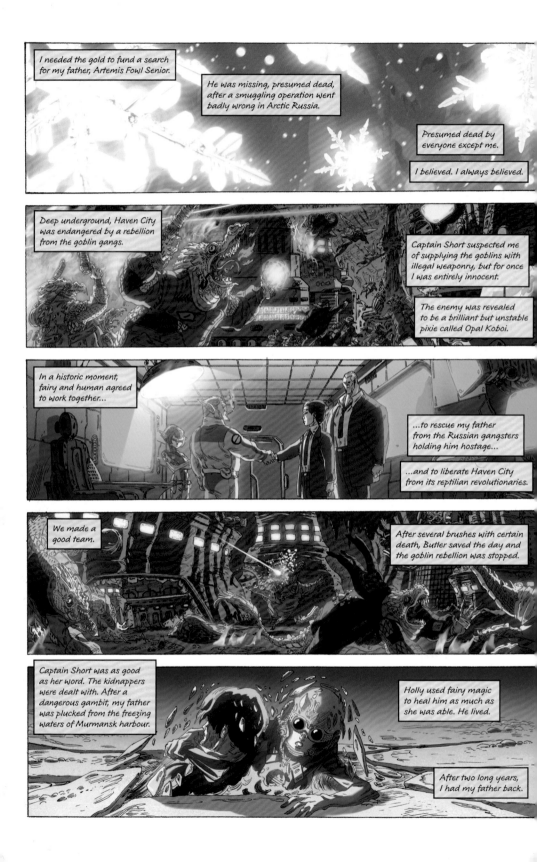

I needed the gold to fund a search for my father, Artemis Fowl Senior.

He was missing, presumed dead, after a smuggling operation went badly wrong in Arctic Russia.

Presumed dead by everyone except me.

I believed. I always believed.

Deep underground, Haven City was endangered by a rebellion from the goblin gangs.

Captain Short suspected me of supplying the goblins with illegal weaponry, but for once I was entirely innocent.

The enemy was revealed to be a brilliant but unstable pixie called Opal Koboi.

In a historic moment, fairy and human agreed to work together...

...to rescue my father from the Russian gangsters holding him hostage...

...and to liberate Haven City from its reptilian revolutionaries.

We made a good team.

After several brushes with certain death, Butler saved the day and the goblin rebellion was stopped.

Captain Short was as good as her word. The kidnappers were dealt with. After a dangerous gambit, my father was plucked from the freezing waters of Murmansk harbour.

Holly used fairy magic to heal him as much as she was able. He lived.

After two long years, I had my father back.

Captain Short and I reached an understanding.

YOU KEEP IT, TO REMIND YOU.

REMIND ME?

THAT DEEP BENEATH THE LAYERS OF DEVIOUSNESS, THERE IS A SPARK OF DECENCY.

PERHAPS YOU COULD BLOW ON THAT SPARK OCCASIONALLY.

Captain Short left me with a gold coin and my memories of the fairy people intact.

While my father has been recovering in a hospital bed in Helsinki, I have busied myself with other schemes.

I sold the Pyramids to a Western businessman.

I forged the lost diaries of Leonardo da Vinci.

GsB auction house

24   08

But my freedom to plot is almost at an end.

My father will soon awake and take back control of the Fowl finances.

With two parents back in Fowl Manor, conducting any illegal ventures undetected may well prove impossible.

Time then for one last brilliant scheme.

After stealing fairy gold, saving their hidden civilization, and rescuing my father, I find myself still hungry for adventure and profit.

It was time for something big.

It was time for lunch....

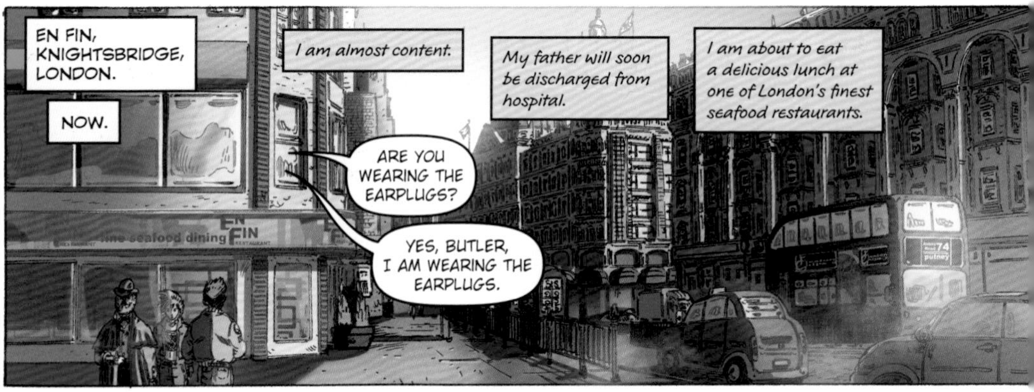
EN FIN, KNIGHTSBRIDGE, LONDON.
NOW.
I am almost content.
My father will soon be discharged from hospital.
I am about to eat a delicious lunch at one of London's finest seafood restaurants.
ARE YOU WEARING THE EARPLUGS?
YES, BUTLER, I AM WEARING THE EARPLUGS.

CHAPTER 1: THE CUBE

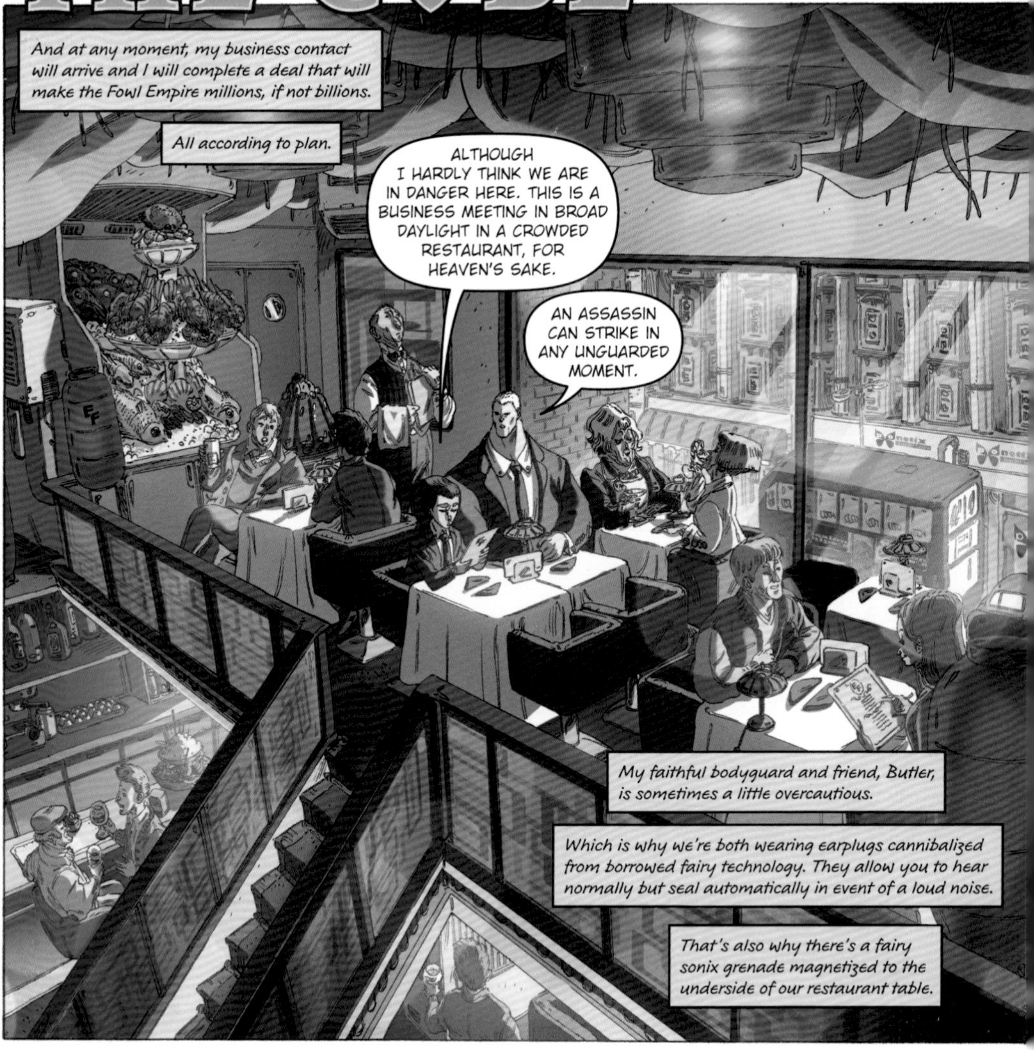
And at any moment, my business contact will arrive and I will complete a deal that will make the Fowl Empire millions, if not billions.
All according to plan.
ALTHOUGH I HARDLY THINK WE ARE IN DANGER HERE. THIS IS A BUSINESS MEETING IN BROAD DAYLIGHT IN A CROWDED RESTAURANT, FOR HEAVEN'S SAKE.
AN ASSASSIN CAN STRIKE IN ANY UNGUARDED MOMENT.
My faithful bodyguard and friend, Butler, is sometimes a little overcautious.
Which is why we're both wearing earplugs cannibalized from borrowed fairy technology. They allow you to hear normally but seal automatically in event of a loud noise.
That's also why there's a fairy sonix grenade magnetized to the underside of our restaurant table.

ANYWAY, BUTLER, WHO COULD POSSIBLY HAVE A MOTIVE TO KILL ME?

THEY MIGHT NOT BE AFTER *YOU*, ARTEMIS.

REMEMBER, JON SPIRO IS A POWERFUL MAN. HE'S MOST LIKELY MADE MANY ENEMIES OVER THE YEARS. WE COULD GET CAUGHT IN A CROSSFIRE.

Butler is right.

Jon Spiro is just the kind of man to attract an assassin's bullet.

TOP SECRET

HARDRIVE

SPIRO

A successful I.T. billionaire, with a shady past and alleged mob connections.

HELLO THERE, YOUNG MAN. WOULD YOU LIKE TO SEE THE CHILDREN'S MENU?

NO, MADEMOISELLE, I WOULD NOT.

I HAVE NO DOUBT THE CHILDREN'S MENU ITSELF TASTES BETTER THAN THE MEALS ON IT.

I WOULD LIKE A MEDLEY OF SHARK AND SWORDFISH, PAN-SEARED, ON A BED OF NEW POTATOES. WITH A BOTTLE OF SPRING WATER. IRISH.

Y-YES, SIR.

WHAT?

AND YOU WONDER WHO MIGHT WANT TO KILL YOU. MOST OF THE WAITERS IN EUROPE FOR A START.

THAT POOR GIRL WAS ALMOST IN TEARS. IT WOULDN'T HURT YOU TO BE NICE OCCASIONA—

BUTLER, WHAT ARE YOU...OH.

Every head in the restaurant turns to see Jon Spiro, and then quickly looks down again.

He's here.

HEY, LITTLE ARTEMIS FOWL CALLS WITH A PROPOSITION, I'VE BEEN SALIVATING ALL THE WAY ACROSS THE ATLANTIC.

MISTER SPIRO, THANK YOU FOR COMING.

I shake his hand. His jewellery jangles like a rattlesnake's tail.

Our bodyguards size each other up.

ARNO BLUNT. I'VE HEARD OF YOU.

BUTLER. ONE OF THE BUTLERS. I HEAR YOU GUYS ARE THE BEST. THAT'S WHAT I *HEAR*.

LET'S HOPE YOU DON'T HAVE TO FIND OUT.

WOULD YOU LIKE TO SEE A MENU?

NO, I DON'T EAT MUCH ANY MORE. PILLS AND LIQUIDS MOSTLY.

GUT PROBLEMS.

SO WHAT HAVE YOU GOT FOR ME, MASTER FOWL?

VERY WELL. TO BUSINESS THEN. WHAT I AM ABOUT TO SHOW YOU IS GOING TO CHANGE THE WORLD.

REALLY?

Now that the moment is here, I suddenly feel very, very uneasy.

I open the box.

WHAT AM I LOOKING AT, KID?

THE FUTURE, MISTER SPIRO. AHEAD OF SCHEDULE.

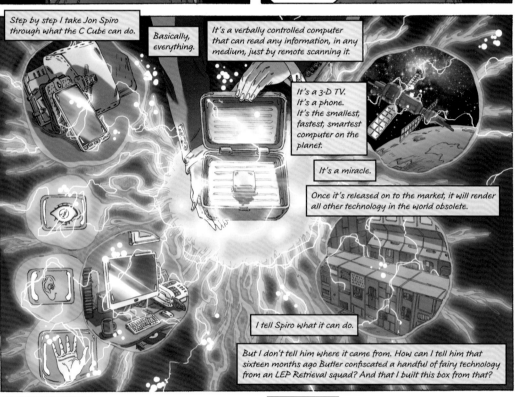

Step by step I take Jon Spiro through what the C Cube can do.

Basically, everything.

It's a verbally controlled computer that can read any information, in any medium, just by remote scanning it.

It's a 3-D TV. It's a phone. It's the smallest, fastest, smartest computer on the planet.

It's a miracle.

Once it's released on to the market, it will render all other technology in the world obsolete.

I tell Spiro what it can do.

But I don't tell him where it came from. How can I tell him that sixteen months ago Butler confiscated a handful of fairy technology from an LEP Retrieval squad? And that I built this box from that?

Of course, Jon Spiro thinks it's a con.

I hack into his encrypted phone, and then into his company's payroll.

Jon Spiro doesn't think it's a con any more.

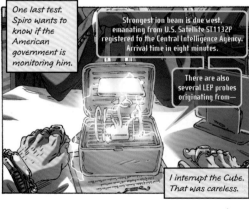

One last test. Spiro wants to know if the American government is monitoring him.

Strongest ion beam is due west, emanating from U.S. Satellite ST1132P registered to the Central Intelligence Agency. Arrival time in eight minutes.

There are also several LEP probes originating from—

I interrupt the Cube. That was careless.

I just nearly exposed my subterranean friends to exactly the kind of man who would exploit them. That fact distracts me.

YOU LISTENING, KID? WE'VE GOT EIGHT MINUTES. LET'S GET DOWN TO THE NITTY-GRITTY. HOW MUCH FOR THE BOX?

FIRST, IT'S A CUBE. SECOND, IT'S NOT FOR SALE.

NOT FOR SALE?!

I'M OFFERING YOU TWELVE MONTHS. FOR THE RIGHT PRICE, I'M PREPARED TO KEEP MY CUBE OFF THE MARKET WHILE YOU SELL YOUR COMPUTER STOCKS AND INVEST THE MONEY IN FOWL INDUSTRIES.

THERE IS NO FOWL INDUSTRIES.

THERE WILL BE.

I feel Butler nudge my leg. He's telling me that it's not a good idea to bait a man like Spiro. He may be right.

YOUR PRICE?

GOLD. ONE METRIC TON.

THAT'S... THAT'S AN AWFUL LOT OF GOLD.

LET'S SAY I DON'T LIKE YOUR TERMS. LET'S SAY THAT I DECIDE TO TAKE YOUR LITTLE GADGET WITH ME RIGHT NOW.

EVEN IF YOU COULD TAKE THE CUBE, IT WOULD BE OF LITTLE USE TO YOU.

THE TECHNOLOGY IS BEYOND ANYTHING YOUR ENGINEERS HAVE EVER SEEN.

I GOT A HELLUVA TEAM AT MY COMPUTER COMPANY, FISSION CHIPS.

THEY'D FIGURE IT OUT EVENTUALLY.

PARDON ME IF I AM UNIMPRESSED BY YOUR "HELLUVA TEAM".

THUS FAR YOU HAVE BEEN TRAILING SEVERAL YEARS BEHIND PHONETIX AND MYISHI CORP.

This time, Butler squeezes my knee. Maybe I have gone too far.

LISTEN, KID, I LIKE YOU. IN A COUPLE OF YEARS, YOU COULD HAVE BEEN JUST LIKE ME. BUT HAVE YOU EVER PUT A GUN TO SOMEBODY'S HEAD AND PULLED THE TRIGGER?

I DIDN'T THINK SO.

SOMETIMES THAT'S WHAT IT TAKES. GUTS. AND YOU DON'T HAVE THEM.

It suddenly strikes me that this is not going according to plan.

MISTER SPIRO, YOU CANNOT BE SERIOUS. WE ARE IN A PUBLIC PLACE, SURROUNDED BY CIVILIANS, IN BROAD DAYLIGHT. YOUR MAN CANNOT HOPE TO COMPETE WITH BUTLER.

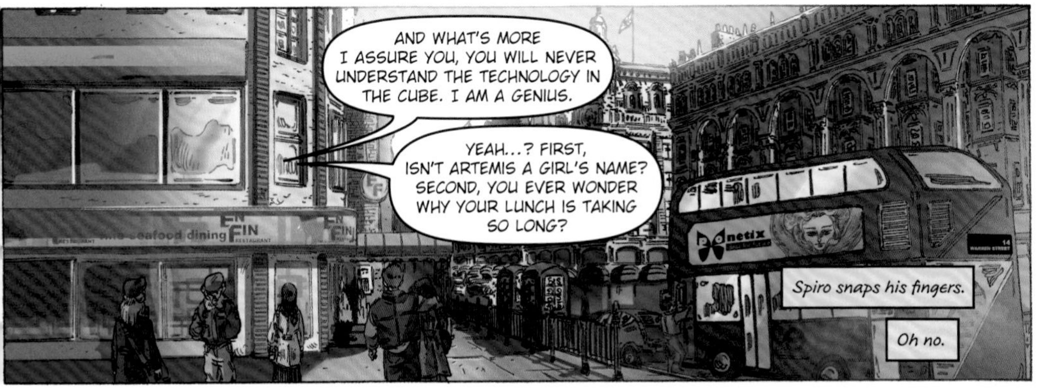
AND WHAT'S MORE I ASSURE YOU, YOU WILL NEVER UNDERSTAND THE TECHNOLOGY IN THE CUBE. I AM A GENIUS.
YEAH...? FIRST, ISN'T ARTEMIS A GIRL'S NAME? SECOND, YOU EVER WONDER WHY YOUR LUNCH IS TAKING SO LONG?
Spiro snaps his fingers.
Oh no.

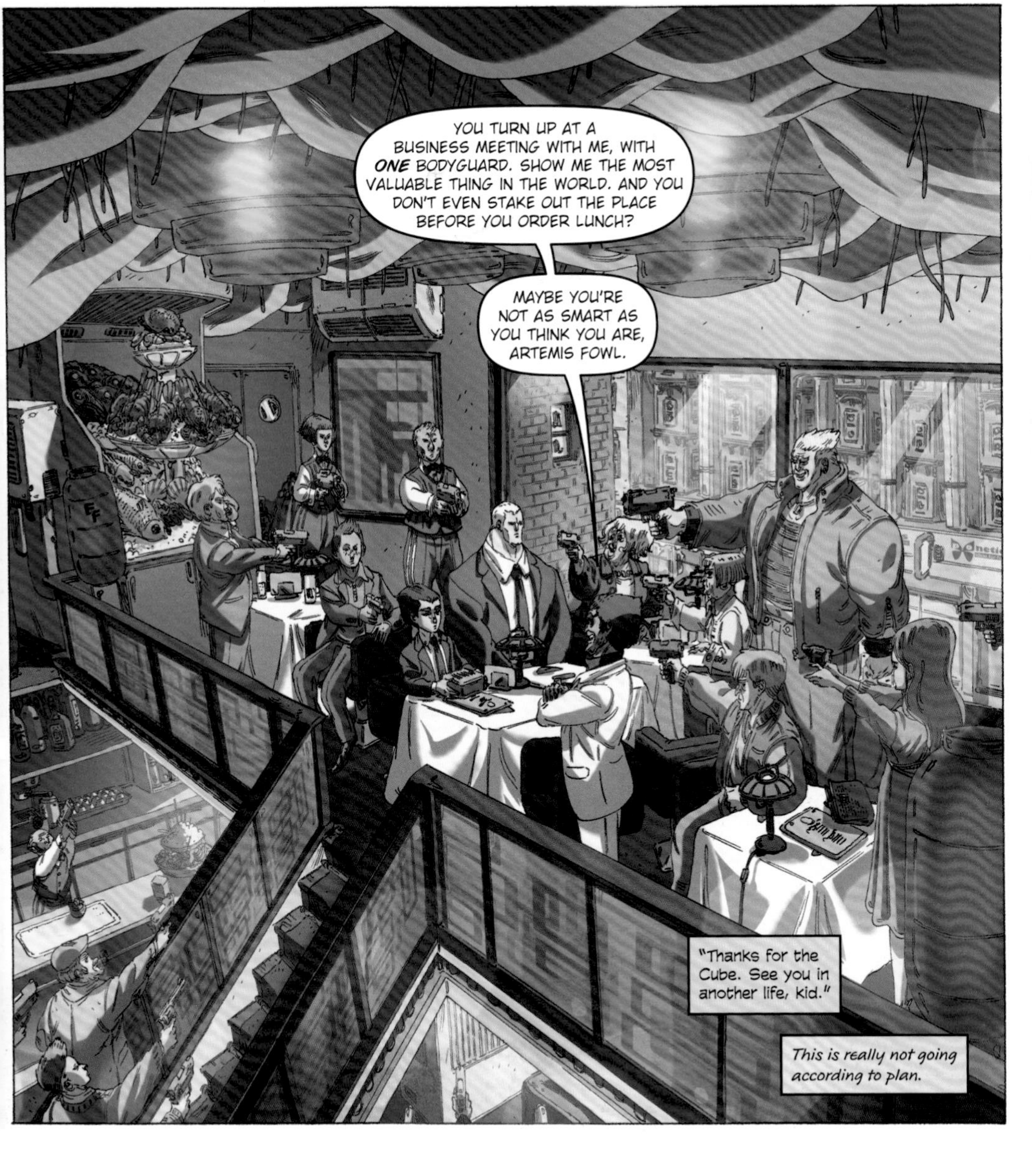
YOU TURN UP AT A BUSINESS MEETING WITH ME, WITH ONE BODYGUARD. SHOW ME THE MOST VALUABLE THING IN THE WORLD. AND YOU DON'T EVEN STAKE OUT THE PLACE BEFORE YOU ORDER LUNCH?
MAYBE YOU'RE NOT AS SMART AS YOU THINK YOU ARE, ARTEMIS FOWL.
"Thanks for the Cube. See you in another life, kid."
This is really not going according to plan.

Spiro leaves before the satellite surveillance beam gets here.

I try to think of a way out for us. There's always a way out, but one won't come.

NOW, LADIES AND GENTLEMEN, I'M SURE WE CAN COME TO SOME ARRANGEMENT.

QUIET, ARTEMIS!

It takes a moment for my brain to process the fact that Butler just ordered me to be silent.

THESE PEOPLE ARE PROFESSIONALS. THEY ARE NOT TO BE BARGAINED WITH.

YOU GOT THAT RIGHT, BUTLER. WE'RE HERE TO KILL YOU. I CAN'T BELIEVE YOU TWO FELL FOR THIS, MAN. YOU MUST BE GETTING OLD.

Maybe Butler is getting old, but now there was an excellent chance he wouldn't be getting any older.

OKAY, BLUNT. YOU AND ME. ONE-ON-ONE.

VERY NOBLE. BUT IF YOU THINK I'M GOING TO RISK YOUR GETTING OUT OF HERE THEN YOU'RE CRAZY.

THIS IS AN UNCOMPLICATED DEAL. I SHOOT YOU. YOU DIE. NO FACE-OFF. NO DUEL.

My brain seems to shut down. The usual stream of ideas dries up. I'm going to die. We're going to die.

Butler's saying something. I decide to listen....

RICHARD OF YORK GAVE BATTLE IN VAIN...

I KNOW THAT. THAT'S ONE OF THOSE MEMORY TRICKS.

I know it too. It's virtually the entire verbal detonation code for the fairy sonix grenade underneath the table.

IT HELPS YOU REMEMBER THE COLOURS OF THE...

I let my jaw go slack and relax my muscles.

...RAINBOW.

"Rainbow."
The final word.

The grenade detonates, sending a solid wall of sound charging through the building.

It blows out windows.

It blows out eardrums.

There is no smoke or flames, but everyone within a ten-metre radius not wearing earplugs is now either unconscious or in severe pain.

As I'm thrown backwards I feel myself caught, safe, in Butler's bear hug.

Butler has saved us again.

I see Butler survey the room.

Spiro's people were down. All of them.

The lucky ones had hit partitions and went straight through. The unlucky ones hit solid bricks and didn't.

WELL DONE, BUTLER. YOU KNOW, WE REALLY MUST TALK ABOUT RAISING YOUR SALARY.

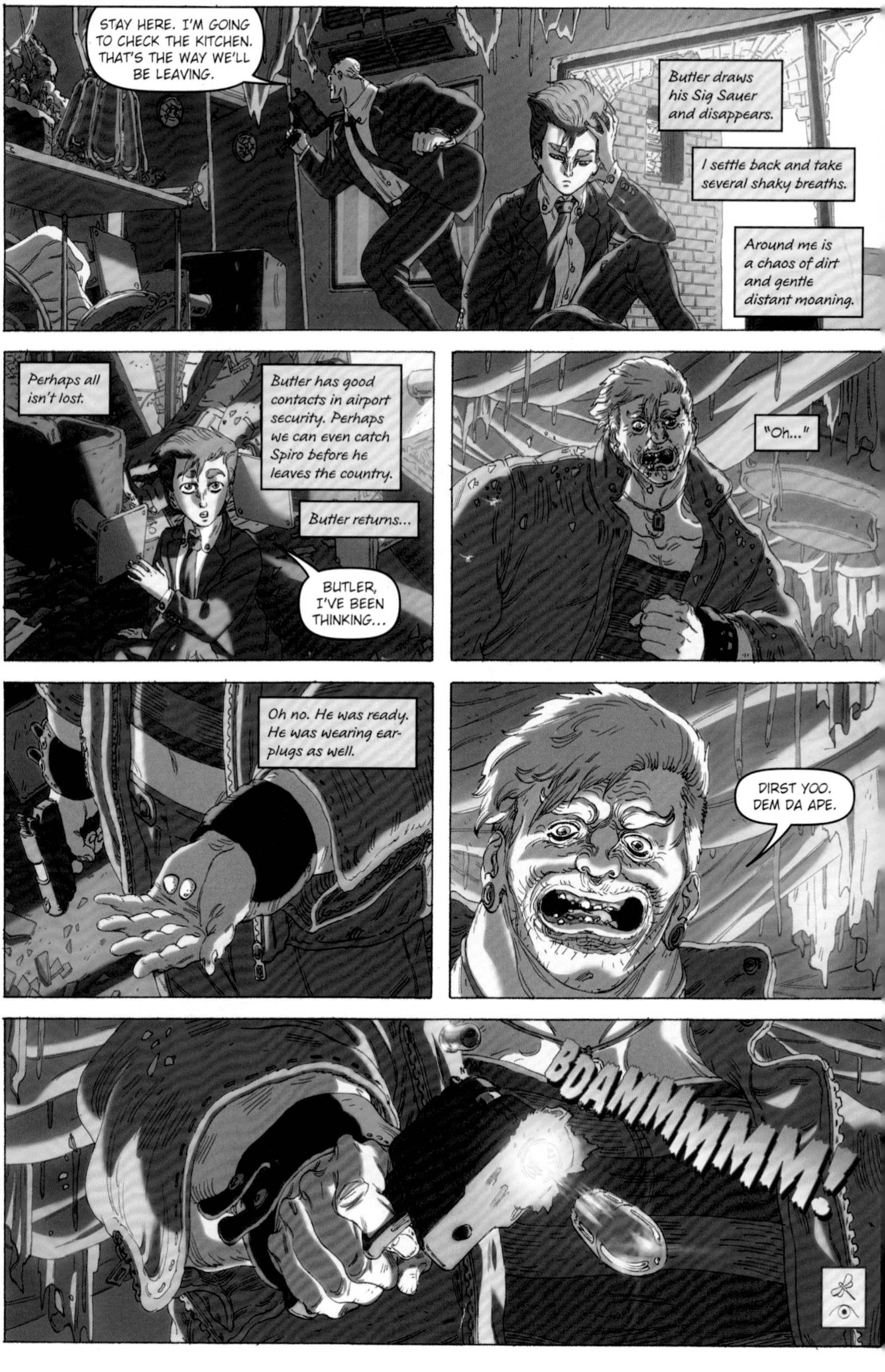
STAY HERE. I'M GOING TO CHECK THE KITCHEN. THAT'S THE WAY WE'LL BE LEAVING.
Butler draws his Sig Sauer and disappears.
I settle back and take several shaky breaths.
Around me is a chaos of dirt and gentle distant moaning.
Perhaps all isn't lost.
Butler has good contacts in airport security. Perhaps we can even catch Spiro before he leaves the country.
Butler returns...
BUTLER, I'VE BEEN THINKING...
"Oh..."
Oh no. He was ready. He was wearing ear-plugs as well.
DIRST YOO. DEM DA APE.
BDAMMMMMM!

HAVEN CITY,
THE LOWER ELEMENTS.

Months after the goblin rebellion and we're still cleaning up the leftovers.

YOU READY, CORPORAL KELP? THE CALL SAID FOUR SUSPECTS INSIDE. LET'S BE CAREFUL, OKAY?

TOO RIGHT. I GOT A TERRIBLE HANGNAIL CUFFING THAT LAST GOBLIN. REALLY NASTY.

My name is Holly Short. I'm a captain in the LEP Reconnaissance squad.

CHAPTER 2:
LOCKDOWN

Usually my job is to fly to the surface on the trail of fairies who venture aboveground without a visa.

I find them and return them underground, where the fairy races have been hiding since Mud Men learned to talk.

Usually...

But now, I'm stuck partnered with Corporal Grub Kelp and assigned to Operation Mop-Up.

THEY'VE EATEN MY ENTIRE STOCK. EVERYTHING! I DIDN'T KNOW WHETHER TO CALL THE COPS, OR LOWER THEM INTO THE DEEP-FAT FRYER.

YOU DID THE RIGHT THING, SIR. IN GENERAL, DEEP-FRYING GOBLINS IS NEVER THE ANSWER.

I can't believe I just said that with a straight face.

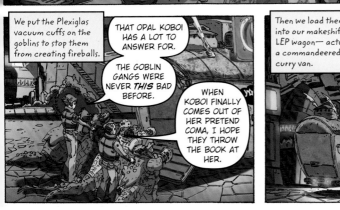

We put the Plexiglas vacuum cuffs on the goblins to stop them from creating fireballs.

THAT OPAL KOBOI HAS A LOT TO ANSWER FOR.

THE GOBLIN GANGS WERE NEVER *THIS* BAD BEFORE.

WHEN KOBOI FINALLY COMES OUT OF HER PRETEND COMA, I HOPE THEY THROW THE BOOK AT HER.

Then we load them into our makeshift LEP wagon— actually a commandeered curry van.

YOU KNOW, HOLLY...I ONLY WISH I'D HAD THE CHANCE TO TACKLE OPAL MYSELF...

Oh no. I know what's coming. If Grub tells his Butler story again then I may have to punch his lights out.

Focus, Holly. Ignore Grub's droning voice. Focus on Haven City—this is why you do your job.

Tens of thousands of fairies all living deep underground.

Tens of thousands of fairies, sprites, dwarfs and even goblins, all relying on the LEP to keep them safe and secret from the prying eyes of humans.

All relying on you...

THE ARGON CLINIC

for your peace of mind

HOLLY, DID I EVER TELL YOU THE STORY OF HOW I FACED DOWN THE HUMAN, BUTLER, DURING THE SIEGE OF FOWL MANOR?

MANY, MANY TIMES.

WOULD YOU LIKE TO HEAR IT AGAIN?

NO.

ALL RIGHT, THEN, JUST FOR YOU. I REMEMBER IT WELL. IT WAS A VERY, VERY DARK NIGHT....

And then suddenly every light in the city goes out right in front of us. Light after light after light.

I DIDN'T DO *THAT*, DID I?

I DON'T THINK SO, GRUB. THE CITY JUST WENT DARK.

There are only three reasons why a lockdown would happen.

Flood.

Quarantine.

The sunstrips overhead fade to black.

The magnastrips' power dries up and our car shudders to a halt.

This is a lockdown. And this is serious.

Or discovery by humans.

I look around. Nobody's drowning. Nobody's sick.

So it must be true—the Mud People are coming.

This could be the end of everything.

HOLLY!

Oh no. The goblins are trying to burn their way out.

The power's off, so their vacuum-sealed handcuffs have popped open.

They're blasting the roof. Idiots.

Goblins. Evolution's little joke. Pick the dumbest creature on the planet and give them the ability to conjure fire.

STOP! WHAT ARE YOU DOING?!

I KNOW YOU WANT TO ESCAPE, BUT YOU KEEP THROWING FIREBALLS AT THE ROOF AND IT'LL COLLAPSE ON YOU!

YOU THINK WE'RE STUPID, ELF? WE'RE GONNA BURN CLEAN THROUGH.

LISTEN, GOBLIN. YOU ARE STUPID. LET'S JUST ACCEPT THAT AND MOVE ON.

YOU'RE ABOUT TO BRING THE ROOF DOWN ON YOURSELVES! YOU'LL ALL BE KILLED!

GET LOST, ELF!

WHOOOOSSSHHH!

The fire extinguisher hasn't kicked in because of the power cut. I'll have to trigger it manually.

I'm about to tell Grub to get to safety when I realize he already has. Great.

WHOOOOOSSS

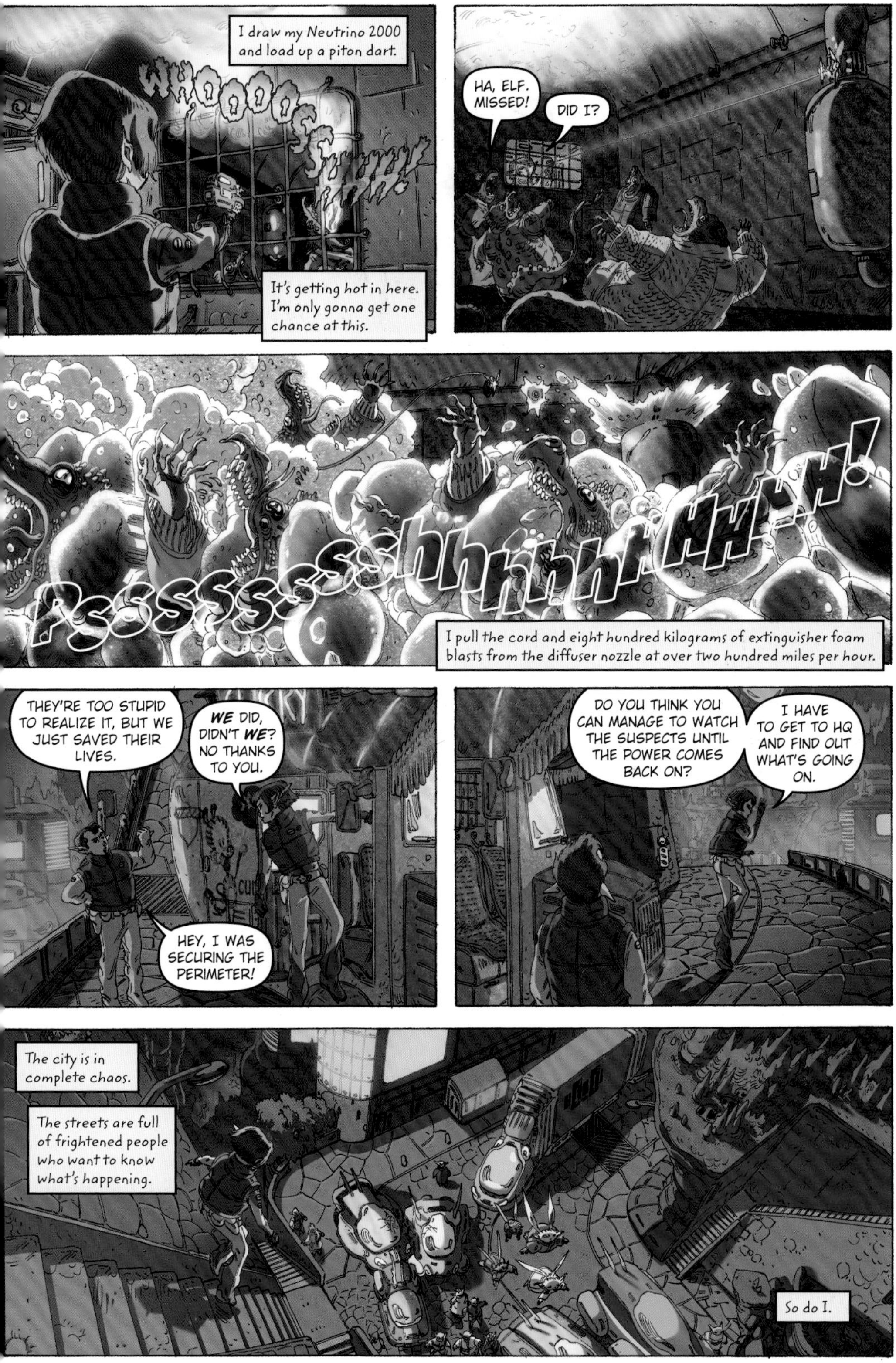
I draw my Neutrino 2000 and load up a piton dart.
WHOOOOSHHH!
It's getting hot in here. I'm only gonna get one chance at this.
HA, ELF. MISSED!
DID I?
PSSSSSS-SSHHHHHH!
I pull the cord and eight hundred kilograms of extinguisher foam blasts from the diffuser nozzle at over two hundred miles per hour.
THEY'RE TOO STUPID TO REALIZE IT, BUT WE JUST SAVED THEIR LIVES.
WE DID, DIDN'T WE? NO THANKS TO YOU.
HEY, I WAS SECURING THE PERIMETER!
DO YOU THINK YOU CAN MANAGE TO WATCH THE SUSPECTS UNTIL THE POWER COMES BACK ON?
I HAVE TO GET TO HQ AND FIND OUT WHAT'S GOING ON.
The city is in complete chaos.
The streets are full of frightened people who want to know what's happening.
So do I.

I push through the crowd around Police Plaza and race inside.

AAAH, GOOD. THE LAST CAPTAIN. SIT DOWN, PLEASE, CAPTAIN SHORT.

The room is packed with captains, commanders and Council members. I take a seat next to Captain Trouble Kelp.

MY LITTLE BROTHER OKAY?

HE GOT A HANGNAIL.

WERE THERE TEARS?

NEARLY.

Foaly comes in and all eyes turn to him.

He's a centaur, a genius, and he's my friend.

Foaly is probably the main reason why humans haven't already discovered our subterranean hideaway.

WHAT HAVE YOU GOT FOR US, FOALY?

I ADVISED CHAIRMAN CAHARTEZ TO INITIATE LOCKDOWN ON THE BASIS OF THESE READINGS.

UHH...I THINK I SPEAK FOR EVERYONE HERE, FOALY, WHEN I SAY THAT ALL I SEE IS LINES AND SQUIGGLES.

OKAY, COMMANDER ROOT. SIMPLY PUT. REALLY SIMPLY. WE GOT PINGED. IS THAT PLAIN ENOUGH?

PINGED?

The room sits in a stunned silence.

Getting pinged was slang for being detected.

Commander Root is first to find his voice.

OKAY, WHO? WHO PINGED US? HUMAN? ALIEN?

THE SIGNAL ORIGINATED IN LONDON, LASTED A FEW SECONDS, AND THEN VANISHED. IT WAS UNTRACEABLE.

BUT IN THOSE FEW SECONDS THEY GOT OUR WHOLE NORTH EUROPE OPERATION. SCOPES, SENTINEL. ALL OUR CAM-CAMS.

THIS IS A CATASTROPHE.

WHAT DOES THIS MEAN FOR THE PEOPLE?

HARD TO SAY, CHAIRMAN CAHARTEZ. THERE ARE BEST- AND WORSE-CASE SCENARIOS.

OUR UNINVITED GUEST COULD LEARN ALL ABOUT US WHENEVER HE WISHES AND DO WITH OUR CIVILIZATION WHAT HE WILL.

AND THE BEST-CASE SCENARIO?

THAT *WAS* THE BEST-CASE SCENARIO.

As always, Commander Root takes charge.

OKAY, HERE'S WHAT WE DO. FOALY, YOU USE YOUR TECH STUFF TO GET AS MUCH INFO FROM THAT "PING" AS YOU CAN. WHO WAS IT? WHAT DID THEY USE?

HOLLY?

WHAT CAN I DO, SIR?

YOU HAVE MORE EXPERIENCE IN DEALING WITH HUMANS THAN ANY OTHER FAIRY ON THE FORCE.

I NEED YOU TO GO TOPSIDE AND WAIT. IF WE GET PINGED AGAIN, I WANT SOMEONE ON SITE READY TO GO.

WILL YOU DO IT? THE FUTURE OF OUR CIVILIZATION COULD DEPEND ON YOU.

OF COURSE I'LL DO IT, COMMANDER. WHEN DO I LEAVE?

I feel the heavy weight of responsibility settle on my shoulders.

This "future of our civilization" thing was happening more and more lately.

EN FIN, KNIGHTSBRIDGE.

SIXTY-FIVE SECONDS AFTER SONIC DETONATION.

GOOD. CIVILIANS ALL UNCONSCIOUS. THIS IS OUR EXIT ROUTE.

CHAPTER 3: OⅡ ÍCE

NOW TO GET ARTEMIS....

THE BODYGUARD'S PRIMARY FUNCTION, BUTLER, IS ALWAYS TO PROTECT HIS PRINCIPAL. THE PRINCIPAL CANNOT BE SHOT IF YOU ARE STANDING IN FRONT OF HIM.

ARTEMIS...

DIRST YOO. DEM DA APE.

"NOOOO!"

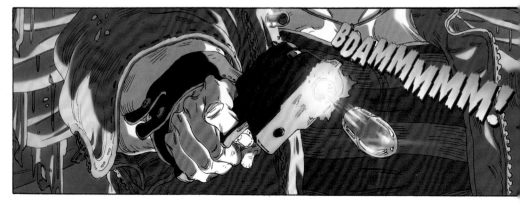

BDAMMMMM!

Butler comes from nowhere.

OOOOMPH UGH!

CCCRASHHHHH!

YOU'RE DEAD NOW....

Butler fires in the direction of the voice, and then I lose consciousness.

AAAUUNGH!

BDAM!

PHEEEEEUUUUU

-uuuuuuhh-
-ugnh?-

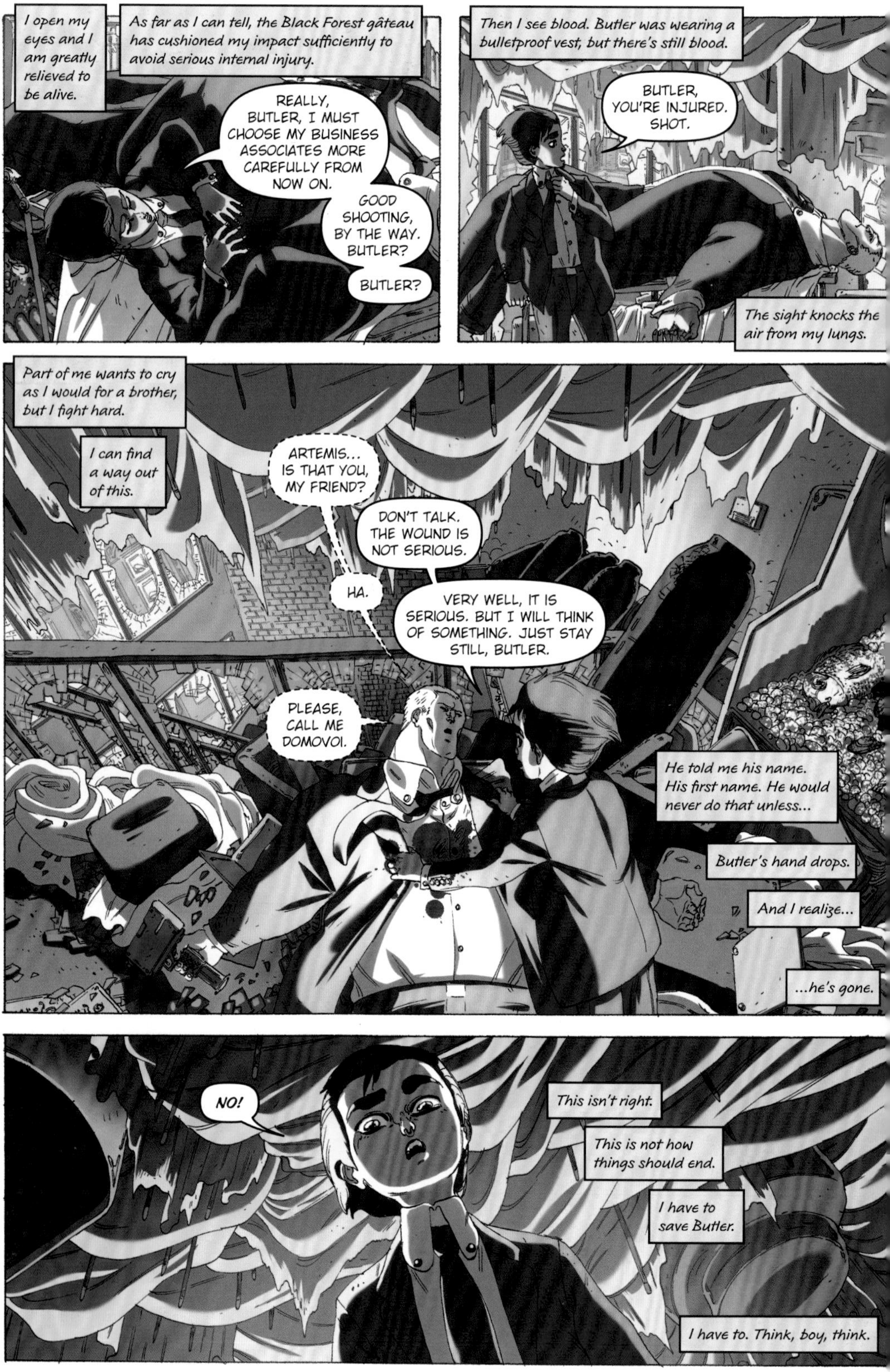
I open my eyes and I am greatly relieved to be alive.
As far as I can tell, the Black Forest gâteau has cushioned my impact sufficiently to avoid serious internal injury.
REALLY, BUTLER, I MUST CHOOSE MY BUSINESS ASSOCIATES MORE CAREFULLY FROM NOW ON.
GOOD SHOOTING, BY THE WAY. BUTLER?
BUTLER?
Then I see blood. Butler was wearing a bulletproof vest, but there's still blood.
BUTLER, YOU'RE INJURED. SHOT.
The sight knocks the air from my lungs.
Part of me wants to cry as I would for a brother, but I fight hard.
I can find a way out of this.
ARTEMIS... IS THAT YOU, MY FRIEND?
DON'T TALK. THE WOUND IS NOT SERIOUS.
HA.
VERY WELL, IT IS SERIOUS. BUT I WILL THINK OF SOMETHING. JUST STAY STILL, BUTLER.
PLEASE, CALL ME DOMOVOI.
He told me his name. His first name. He would never do that unless...
Butler's hand drops.
And I realize...
...he's gone.
NO!
This isn't right.
This is not how things should end.
I have to save Butler.
I have to. Think, boy, think.

I need to think about the bigger picture.

EVERYTHING JUST WENT "POP".

I NEVER DID LIKE FISH.

Butler almost died once before. Mauled by a troll. But Holly Short saved him using her fairy magic.

Now Butler has perhaps four minutes before his brain shuts down. Time is the enemy here.

I need to buy some more time. Or maybe steal some.

Think, boy, think.

Use what's around you.

Ovens. Sinks. Ice. Utensils. Lobsters.

Ice.

I can't stop time, but perhaps I can halt Butler's passage through it.

Cryogenics. My only hope.

Freezing a body until medicine has evolved enough to revive.

Or in this case, freezing it until I can get fairy help.

I quickly evict the salmon and sea bass.

Then I lever Butler's bulk into the steaming ice.

From outside, I can hear the sound of emergency vehicles getting closer.

I'LL BE BACK, OLD FRIEND. SLEEP WELL.

I adjust the thermostat to four below zero to avoid tissue damage and leave before the police arrive.

I leave through the rear door, mingle with the crowd and walk away.

I don't look back.

The police often have someone photographing the crowd.

Even though it's Butler, I don't look back.

The waitress brings me a pot of Earl Grey tea and I get to work.

"Detective Inspector Justin Barre please."

"Speaking."

THIS IS ARTEMIS FOWL.

HELLO, ARTEMIS, HOW ARE YOU? HOW'S THE BIG GUY?

NOT WELL. NOT WELL AT ALL, I'M AFRAID. BUTLER NEEDS A FAVOUR. A BIG FAVOUR.

ANYTHING FOR BUTLER. MY CAREER AND MY LIFE WOULD HAVE ENDED AT SERGEANT IF IT HADN'T BEEN FOR BUTLER.

I tell him as much as I dare.

"That's a strange request, Artemis. Even for you. What's in the freezers?"

I explain that for Butler, this is a matter of life or death.

ICE AGE CRYOGENICS INSTITUTE, OFF HARLEY STREET, LONDON.

I NEED TO RENT ONE OF YOUR CRYOGENIC UNITS URGENTLY, PLEASE.

I'M AFRAID WE ARE QUITE BOOKED UP.

I CAN OFFER YOU A HUNDRED THOUSAND POUNDS IN CASH.

WHAT COLOUR WOULD YOU PREFER, SIR?

The pieces to save Butler are falling into place. Now all I need is Holly.

SHUTTLEPORT 51, THE LOWER ELEMENTS.

One flash of my Recon badge opens a route right through to the surface.

There are no magma flares scheduled, so I'm on the next commercial shuttle flight.

DOES EVERYONE HAVE THEIR SONG SHEETS READY?

The entire Brotherhood of Bog—food worshippers— are on their annual picnic aboveground.

‹BURP!›

Lucky me.

PIZZA, PIZZA, FILL UP YOUR FACE, THE THICKER THE PASTRY, THE BETTER THE BASE!

There are another hundred and fourteen verses.

Sadly, the blasters kick in at full throttle and I don't get to hear them.

CHUTE EXIT,
STONEHENGE,
WILTSHIRE.

I badge my way past
the customs queue
and take a security
elevator to the surface.

I strap on my wings, and for
the first time in what feels
like forever, I'm free.

Sunset.

Perfect.
My favourite
time of day.

I activate my shield. Now I'm invisible
to all human and mechanical eyes.

Despite the situation, a slow
smile spreads across my face.

This is what I
was born to do.

THESE UNITS COST ALMOST A MILLION APIECE. THE VANS ARE CUSTOM-MADE IN MUNICH; SPECIALLY ARMOURED TOO.

THAT'S VERY, VERY NICE, DOCTOR, BUT CAN IT GO ANY FASTER?

Doctor Lane tries to frown but I don't think there's enough slack skin on her forehead.

We get to the delivery entrance of En Fin, and as promised, there are no police. Except one...

CRYOGENICS? DO YOU THINK YOU CAN DO ANYTHING FOR HIM?

YOU LOOKED IN THE FREEZER THEN?

Doctor Lane's paramedics have five minutes to get Butler out before the regular police return.

YES, AND I'M SORRY I DID. HE WAS A GOOD MAN.

IS A GOOD MAN. I AM NOT READY TO GIVE UP ON HIM YET.

"Who pulled the trigger, Artemis?"

"A hired gun called Arno Blunt."

"Butler saved my life. That bullet was meant for me."

When I see Butler wheeled out, it's everything I can do to look Barre in the eye.

ARTEMIS, ARE YOU SURE ABOUT THIS?

DETECTIVE INSPECTOR, I GUARANTEE YOU THAT BY TOMORROW BUTLER WILL BE ALIVE AND KICKING. I'LL HAVE HIM PHONE YOU WHEN HE IS.

ANY SURGEON WHO CAN FIX THAT WOUND IS A REAL MAGICIAN.

"That's the plan, Detective Inspector. That's the plan."

I head for London.

Doctor Lane prepares Butler.

I slip into Doctor Lane's office and make a very important phone call.

When I return to the van, Doctor Lane is administering glucose injections.

Mobile cryogenic unit.
(Doctor Lane's design.)

Temperature gauge.

-04° C
min -- max --

Cold packs.

"Holly, do you read? This is Foaly.
I've got alarms flashing here.

"We need you to investigate.
Someone in London just made
the strangest phone call."

So I wait.

I've sent Doctor Lane away. And I've made my call.

"People, LEP, magic, Haven, shuttleports, sprites, B'wa Kell, trolls, time-stop, Recon, Atlantis."

I know Foaly monitors human communications, and those keywords should set off ALL his alarms.

I made the call from Doctor Lane's landline instead of my mobile. I'm not sure they'll come if they know it's me.

So I wait.

Not for the first time.

EXCERPT FROM ARTEMIS FOWL'S DIARY. DISK 2. ENCRYPTED.

It has been weeks since Holly Short used her healing magic on my father's battered body.

And still he lies in his Helsinki hospital.

Immobile. Unresponsive.

The doctors cannot understand it. But it's no mystery to me.

Holly's magic has overhauled my father's entire being.

I cannot help but wonder what effect the positive energy will have on his mind.

For sixteen days we sat in my father's hospital room.

Waiting.

On the morning of the seventeenth day, my father's brain waves began to spike.

He simply sat up, rubbed his eyes, and said Mother's name. "Angeline."

Suddenly, I was afraid.

The man whose shoes I had been trying to fill for two years was awake.

Would he live up to my expectations? Would I live up to his?

After such a long time apart. I didn't know what to say.

My father had no such doubts.

ARTY...

I run to his embrace.

YOU'RE A MAN NOW. A YOUNG MAN.

He held me close and I had a father again.

I had my family back together.

At least I thought I had.

There's a sly movement on a roof above. I fix my gaze on the spot, watching through the stolen fairy lens in my glasses.

Crouching in the moonlight is a Recon officer.

Butler's life depends on what happens in the next few seconds.

DON'T SHOOT—PLEASE. I'M UNARMED. AND I NEED YOUR HELP.

The fairy descends towards me.

DON'T BE ALARMED. I AM A FRIEND TO THE PEOPLE.

I KNOW ABOUT YOUR EXISTENCE. I HELPED DEFEAT THE B'WA KELL. MY NAME IS—

I KNOW WHO YOU ARE...ARTEMIS.

HOLLY! IT'S YOU.

I PRESUME YOU MADE THE CALL? WHY DIDN'T YOU USE YOUR OWN PHONE?

I COULDN'T BE SURE YOU'D COME. YOU MIGHT HAVE THOUGHT IT WAS A TRAP.

LIKE THE TIME YOU SHOT AND KIDNAPPED ME?

YOU'RE NEVER GOING TO LET ME FORGET THAT, ARE YOU?

IN A WORD... NO.

ANYWAY... WHERE'S BUTLER?

The Mud Boy doesn't answer. But his expression tells me exactly why he's summoned me.

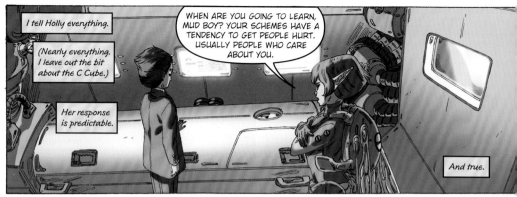

I tell Holly everything.

(Nearly everything. I leave out the bit about the C Cube.)

WHEN ARE YOU GOING TO LEARN, MUD BOY? YOUR SCHEMES HAVE A TENDENCY TO GET PEOPLE HURT. USUALLY PEOPLE WHO CARE ABOUT YOU.

Her response is predictable.

And true.

CAN YOU HEAL HIM?

ME? ARTEMIS, THIS ISN'T LIKE YOUR FATHER. HE WAS JUST INJURED.

I HATE TO SAY IT, BUT BUTLER IS GONE. LONG GONE.

REMEMBER THIS?

"You gave it to me for ensuring your trigger finger got reattached to your hand.

"You said it was to remind me of the spark of decency inside me.

"Well, I'm trying to do something decent now."

PLEASE, HOLLY. I CAN'T JUST LET HIM GO.

IT'S BUTLER....

I look at Artemis and I can't help myself. Butler has saved my life on more than one occasion.

ALL RIGHT, MUD BOY. LET'S SEE WHAT FOALY HAS GOT TO SAY.

I try to compose myself. I have seconds to present a convincing case, or Butler's last chance is gone.

ALL I WANT IS A HEALING, FOALY. I ACCEPT THAT IT MAY NOT WORK, BUT WHAT DOES IT COST TO TRY?

It's not that simple, Mud Boy. Holly is good, but for something like this we'd need a trained team of warlocks.

There may already be damage to the brain tissue.

No. I got his temperature down in minutes. The cranium has been frozen since the incident. The brain is fine. I'm sure.

Foaly doesn't speak for several moments.

I can hear my heart beating.

ARTEMIS, THIS HAS NEVER BEEN DONE ON A HUMAN BEFORE.

I understand.

DO YOU, ARTEMIS? REALLY? WHATEVER EMERGES FROM HIS POD IS YOURS TO CARE FOR. WILL YOU ACCEPT THIS RESPONSIBILITY?

I don't hesitate.

I WILL.

Then it's Holly's decision. If she wants to use her magic and try, it's up to her.

HOLLY... PLEASE. WILL YOU DO IT?

I'LL TRY. NO GUARANTEES, BUT I'LL DO WHAT I CAN.

My knees nearly buckle with relief.

"Holly, tell me. What can I do to help?"

"One thing."

"Of course. Anything."

"Get out. And whatever you see, whatever you hear, don't come in until I call."

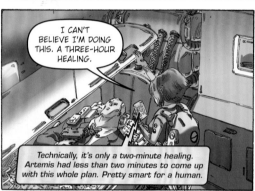

I CAN'T BELIEVE I'M DOING THIS. A THREE-HOUR HEALING.

Technically, it's only a two-minute healing. Artemis had less than two minutes to come up with this whole plan. Pretty smart for a human.

ARE YOU REALLY SURE THIS IS A GOOD IDEA, FOALY?

I wish we had time for discussion, Holly. But every second costs our old friend a couple of brain cells.

Show me the wound.

UGH! AND THERE ARE FIBRES TRAPPED IN THERE. KEVLAR, I'D SAY.

That's all we need. Complications.

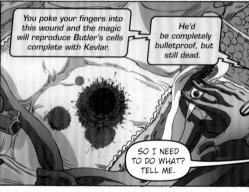

You poke your fingers into this wound and the magic will reproduce Butler's cells complete with Kevlar.

He'd be completely bulletproof, but still dead.

SO I NEED TO DO WHAT? TELL ME.

I work fast.

Okay. Surgery for morons it is. You need to make a new wound—the other pectoral—and let the magic spread from there.

So use your Neutrino 2000 on a low setting to melt him down a little.

Be ready, Holly. Butler needs to be healed before oxygen gets to his brain. Otherwise it's over.

The colour returns to Butler as the ice melts around his body.

"Now get your hands in deep and give it every drop of magic that you've got."

"Don't just let it flow; push the magic out. Do it now."

-04° C
min — max —

I've never liked this bit—no matter how many healings you perform—sticking your fingers into other people's insides.

HEAL!

"More, Holly. Another shot."

I push harder.

Then harder still. (This is Butler.)

I feel the heart start.

That's the easy bit.

"It's starting, Holly. Now stand back."

Now that my plan is actually in progress, doubts begin to chew at the edges of my mind.

What if Butler isn't himself afterwards? After all, my father had been undeniably different.

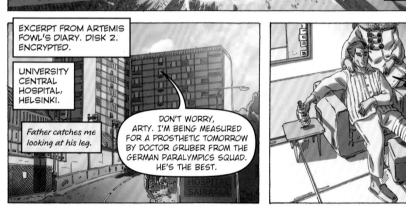

EXCERPT FROM ARTEMIS FOWL'S DIARY. DISK 2. ENCRYPTED.

UNIVERSITY CENTRAL HOSPITAL, HELSINKI.

Father catches me looking at his leg.

DON'T WORRY, ARTY. I'M BEING MEASURED FOR A PROSTHETIC TOMORROW BY DOCTOR GRUBER FROM THE GERMAN PARALYMPICS SQUAD. HE'S THE BEST.

I'M GOING TO ASK HIM FOR SOMETHING SPORTY.

MAYBE WITH SPEED STRIPES.

A joke. That wasn't like my father.

And there were also other, deeper, changes.

BUT I SEEM TO HAVE FAILED YOU, SON, IF YOU THINK ACCOUNTS AND STOCKS ARE ALL THAT'S IMPORTANT. I'VE FOCUSED TOO MUCH ON BUSINESS IN THE PAST. BUT NOW I WANT A BETTER LIFE FOR US ALL.

YOU WILL FIND THE FAMILY BANK ACCOUNTS ARE HEALTHY, FATHER, AS IS THE STOCK PORTFOLIO. I HAVEN'T FAILED YOU.

WE ARE WHAT'S IMPORTANT.

HE'S LIKE A NEW MAN. NO, NOT A NEW MAN. AN OLD ONE.

THE MAN I FELL IN LOVE WITH AND MARRIED, BEFORE THE FOWL EMPIRE TOOK OVER.

YOUR FATHER'S BACK.

I could not believe what I was hearing.

I was surprised, but not unpleasantly so.

What had Holly's magic done to him?

I am suddenly yanked back to the present.

SKRANNRUMP!

"Get in there, Holly!"

WHAT?

"The magic is spreading up his spinal column. Hold his head still for the healing, or any damaged cells could be replicated."

"Hold him. Hold him steady!"

"Here it comes...."

"Brace yourself, Holly!"

KA-BOOOOOM!

"You did it, Holly. He's alive."

"Yes, but...Oh, gods. Artemis is not going to like this."

I do not panic.

Much.

DID IT WORK? IS HE ALIVE?

"He's alive, Artemis, but my magic wasn't enough. The healing used up some of Butler's own life force."

"About fifteen years' worth, by the looks of it."

IF IT'S ANY CONSOLATION, HE'LL PROBABLY LIVE LONGER THAN HE WOULD HAVE NATURALLY.

HE'S ALIVE.

AS LONG AS YOU DON'T GET HIM SHOT AGAIN.

YOU NEED TO GET HIM OUT OF HERE. AND I NEED TO GET BACK TO MY MISSION.

HAVEN CITY WAS PROBED THIS MORNING AND I HAVE TO FIND OUT HOW AND WHY.

CAPTAIN SHORT. HOLLY—ABOUT THAT PROBE...I...I THINK IT MIGHT HAVE BEEN ME.

OKAY, MUD BOY. LET'S TAKE THIS SOMEWHERE PRIVATE.

THE IRISH SEA, MIDNIGHT.

Even with Holly's weight-reducing Moonbelt, it's a struggle to get us all in the air.

FOWL MANOR, IRELAND.

We put Butler safely to bed. Then Holly wastes no time.

NOW EXPLAIN YOURSELF, FOWL.

FOALY, RECORD THIS, WOULD YOU? I HAVE A FEELING WE'RE GOING TO WANT TO HEAR IT AGAIN.

Okay, Holly.

GO ON, ARTEMIS.

THIS ENTIRE INCIDENT BEGAN AT A BUSINESS MEETING THIS AFTERNOON WITH JON SPIRO. HE'S AN AMERICAN, ERR, INDUSTRIALIST.

CHECK IT, FOALY.

JON SPIRO...HMMMM. SHADY, EVEN BY HUMAN STANDARDS. HIS COMPANIES ARE ECO-DISASTERS.

HE'S ALSO INTO INDUSTRIAL ESPIONAGE, ABDUCTION, BLACKMAIL, AND HE'S UP TO HIS NECK IN MOB CONNECTIONS. NICE GUY.

WHAT WERE YOU SELLING HIM, ARTEMIS? A MAN LIKE SPIRO DOESN'T CROSS THE ATLANTIC FOR TEA AND MUFFINS.

I WASN'T ACTUALLY SELLING HIM ANYTHING. BUT I DID OFFER TO SUPPRESS SOME REVOLUTIONARY TECHNOLOGY—FOR A PRICE, OF COURSE.

What "revolutionary technology"?

Foaly's voice is cold with fear.

DO YOU REMEMBER THOSE HELMETS BUTLER TOOK FROM THE RETRIEVAL SQUAD?

OH NO.

OH NO... NO...

I DEACTIVATED THE HELMET'S AUTO-DESTRUCT MECHANISMS AND USED THE TECH TO CREATE A HANDHELD SUPERCOMPUTER CALLED THE C CUBE.

AND YOU GAVE FAIRY TECHNOLOGY TO A MAN LIKE JON SPIRO?

I QUITE OBVIOUSLY DIDN'T GIVE IT TO HIM. HE TOOK IT.

WHAT DID YOU THINK WOULD HAPPEN?!

THAT JON SPIRO WAS GOING TO WALK AWAY FROM TECHNOLOGY THAT COULD MAKE HIM THE RICHEST MAN ON THE PLANET?

"So it was your computer that pinged us?"

"Yes. Unintentionally. Spiro asked for surveillance and the C Cube's fairy circuits picked up your LEP equipment."

"That's terrible news, Holly. Haven's deflectors will be useless against our own technology. Sooner or later Spiro will find out about the People."

And if that happens, I can't see a man like him just leaving us alone.

REMIND YOU OF ANYONE?

I AM NOTHING LIKE JON SPIRO. HE'S A COLD-BLOODED KILLER!

GIVE YOURSELF A FEW YEARS. YOU'LL GET THERE.

Okay, Holly, calm down. Let's try to act like professionals.

Step one is to call off the lockdown. Our next priority is to retrieve the Cube before Spiro can unlock its secrets.

WE DO HAVE SOME TIME. THE CUBE IS ENCRYPTED WITH AN ETERNITY CODE. I INVENTED AN ENTIRELY NEW BASE LANGUAGE, SO ANYONE TRYING TO DECODE IT WOULD HAVE NO FRAME OF REFERENCE.

An eternity code. I'm impressed.

BUT I DON'T THINK WE NEED TO GO HUNTING SPIRO. ONCE HE REALIZES THAT I'M ALIVE HE'LL COME LOOKING FOR ME.

AFTER ALL, I'M HIS BEST HOPE OF UNLOCKING THE FULL POTENTIAL OF THE CUBE.

GREAT. SO ANY MOMENT NOW A TEAM OF HIT MEN COULD COME BLASTING IN HERE, LOOKING FOR THE KEY TO YOUR ETERNITY-CODE THING?

IT'S AT TIMES LIKE THESE WE COULD DO WITH SOMEONE LIKE BUTLER AROUND.

THAT IS A VERY GOOD THOUGHT, CAPTAIN. ESPECIALLY AS THERE IS MORE THAN ONE BUTLER IN THE FAMILY. IT'S TIME I MADE A PHONE CALL.

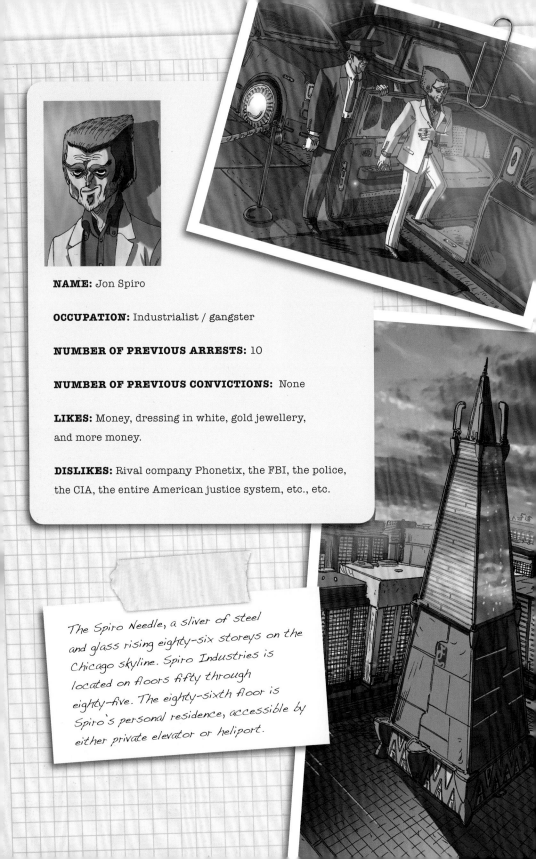

NAME: Jon Spiro

OCCUPATION: Industrialist / gangster

NUMBER OF PREVIOUS ARRESTS: 10

NUMBER OF PREVIOUS CONVICTIONS: None

LIKES: Money, dressing in white, gold jewellery, and more money.

DISLIKES: Rival company Phonetix, the FBI, the police, the CIA, the entire American justice system, etc., etc.

The Spiro Needle, a sliver of steel and glass rising eighty-six storeys on the Chicago skyline. Spiro Industries is located on floors fifty through eighty-five. The eighty-sixth floor is Spiro's personal residence, accessible by either private elevator or heliport.

THE (ALMOST) SECRET DIARY OF JULIET BUTLER.

My training began when I was four.

By the time I was eight, I was a third-dan black belt in seven disciplines.

By eleven, I was beyond belts.

CHAPTER 4: RUNNING IN THE FAMILY

SFAX, TUNISIA, NORTH AFRICA.

I've spent the last six months learning the craft of the bodyguard.

Taught by the same sensei that instructed my brother, Butler.

Six months of training days that started at 5:30 a.m. and never seemed to stop.

And now it all comes down to this.

The final field test.

HURRY. YOU WILL LOSE ME.

IN YOUR DREAMS, MADAME.

Protect Madame Ko as she walks through the city market.

She's trying to distract me with conversation. It won't work. I've got enough distractions to deal with already.

I HAVE VERY GOOD CARPET.

If I pass the test then I get the famous blue diamond tattoo.

YOU COME WITH ME. I SHOW YOU BEST CARPETS.

NO, THANK YOU.

And today, passing the test is all that matters.

This is taking too long. Madame Ko is out of sight.

I GIVE GOOD BARGAIN. BEST RUGS IN SFAX.

I'm losing the principal.

I don't know if he's just an innocent bystander...

WHAT!?

...or if Madame Ko has employed him to get in my way.

Either way, I need him gone.

OMMP!

I have to find Madame Ko or this test is over.

I take off like a sprinter out of the blocks, dodging around the stunned merchants.

Madame Ko can't have gone far.

I can still complete my assignment.... Oh no.

These aren't merchants.

This is no test.

These men are trying to kill my sensei.

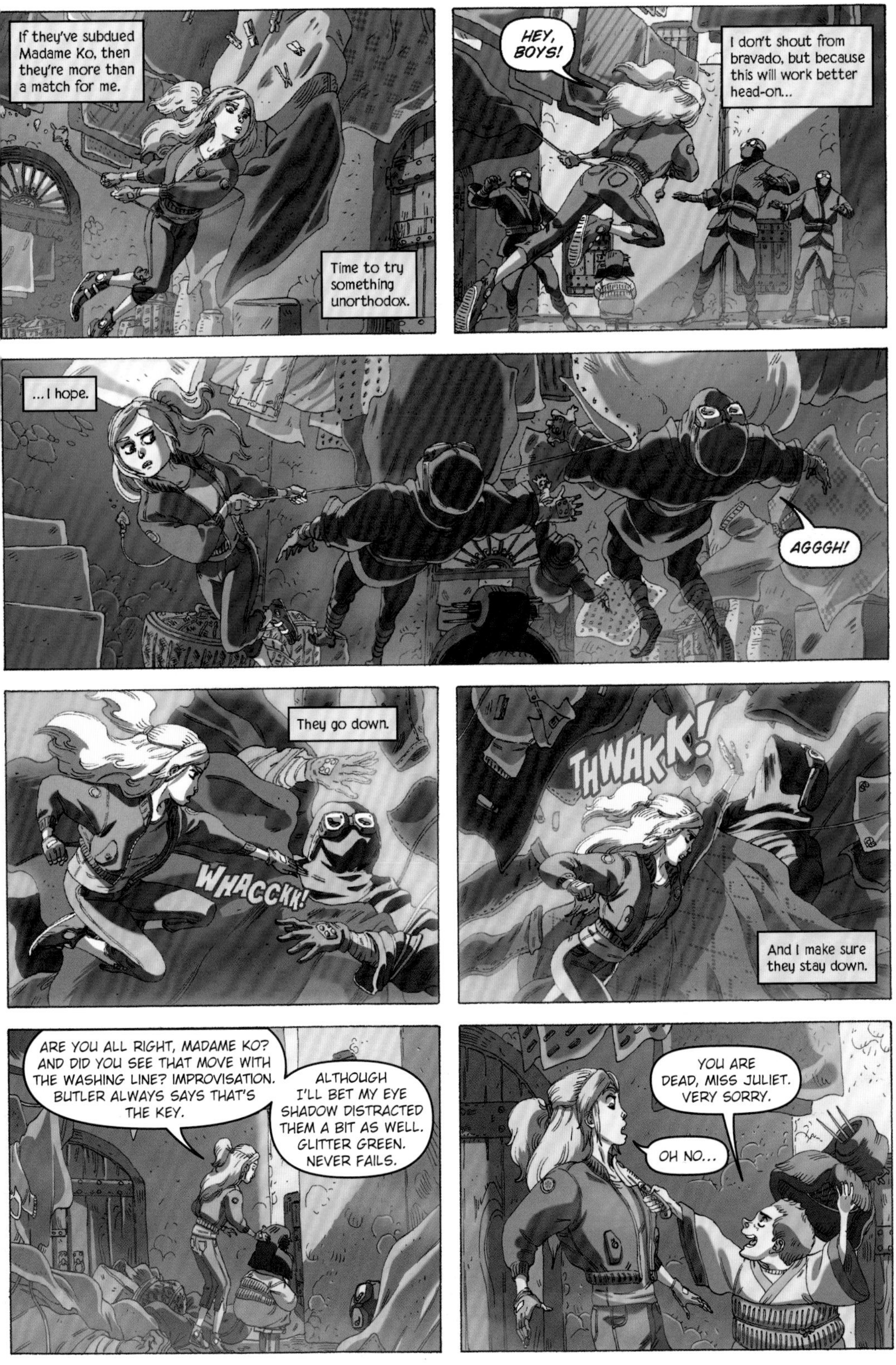
If they've subdued Madame Ko, then they're more than a match for me.
Time to try something unorthodox.
HEY, BOYS!
I don't shout from bravado, but because this will work better head-on...
...I hope.
AGGGH!
They go down.
WHACCKK!
THWAKK!
And I make sure they stay down.
ARE YOU ALL RIGHT, MADAME KO? AND DID YOU SEE THAT MOVE WITH THE WASHING LINE? IMPROVISATION. BUTLER ALWAYS SAYS THAT'S THE KEY.
ALTHOUGH I'LL BET MY EYE SHADOW DISTRACTED THEM A BIT AS WELL. GLITTER GREEN. NEVER FAILS.
YOU ARE DEAD, MISS JULIET. VERY SORRY.
OH NO...

AND IF YOU ARE DEAD, THEN THE PRINCIPAL IS DEAD. AND YOU HAVE FAILED.

USING A DECOY WAS A SLY TRICK, MADAME KO.

WHERE DID YOU MAKE YOUR MISTAKE? THINK FOR ONCE. WHAT SHOULD YOU HAVE DONE?

THE GUY IN THE MARKET. I SHOULD HAVE INCAPACITATED THE MERCHANT IMMEDIATELY.

EXACTLY. HIS WELL-BEING MEANS NOTHING. INSIGNIFICANT, COMPARED TO THE PRINCIPAL'S SAFETY.

BUT I CAN'T JUST HIT ANYONE WHO GETS IN MY WAY.

I KNOW, CHILD. AND THAT IS WHY YOU ARE NOT READY.

YOU HAVE SKILL, BUT NOT FOCUS AND RESOLVE.

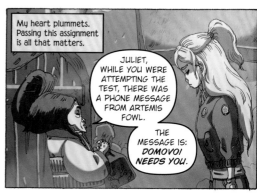

My heart plummets. Passing this assignment is all that matters.

JULIET, WHILE YOU WERE ATTEMPTING THE TEST, THERE WAS A PHONE MESSAGE FROM ARTEMIS FOWL.

THE MESSAGE IS: *DOMOVOI NEEDS YOU.*

YOU MEAN HE SAID...BUTLER NEEDS ME.

BUTLER WOULD NEVER REVEAL HIS NAME TO ARTEMIS. NOT UNLESS...

I'M VERY SORRY. YOU MAY GO, OF COURSE.

And suddenly the test doesn't matter.

It doesn't matter at all.

OKAY, PEARSON, YOU AND THE TECHNICAL DEPARTMENT HAVE HAD THE C CUBE FOR SIX HOURS. WHAT HAVE YOU GOT FOR ME?

ERR...WELL, MISTER SPIRO. IT'S ERR... USELESS.

USELESS?! I'VE SEEN IT IN ACTION. PERHAPS WHAT'S USELESS AROUND HERE IS YOU.

IT...IT UNDOUBTEDLY HAS ENORMOUS POTENTIAL, BUT IT'S ENCRYPTED.

I PUMP TWO HUNDRED MILLION INTO YOUR DEPARTMENT, BUT YOU CAN'T BREAK ONE LOUSY CODE, SET UP BY A KID?

IT'S NOT JUST ANY CODE, SIR. IT'S AN ETERNITY CODE—AN ENCRYPTION BASED ON AN ENTIRELY UNKNOWN LANGUAGE INVENTED BY FOWL. THERE ARE TRILLIONS OF POSSIBLE PERMUTATIONS.

CHAPTER 5: THE METAL MAN AND THE MONKEY

PLEASE DON'T THROW ANY MORE OLIVES AT ME, MISTER SPIRO.

YOU COULD TRY OPENING YOUR MOUTH.

PLEASE, SIR, I HAVE A NOBEL PRIZE.

THE CODE IS UNBREAKABLE. OR NEARLY. IT MIGHT TAKE ME THE REST OF MY CAREER TO CRACK IT.

YEAH? THAT MIGHT BE A LOT SHORTER THAN YOU THINK.

≥gulp≤ I'M VERY SORRY, MISTER SPIRO, BUT IF FOWL IS DEAD, THEN THE SECRETS OF THE C CUBE DIED WITH HIM.

OKAY, DOC. YOU'RE DISMISSED. YOU DON'T WANNA HEAR WHAT'S COMING NEXT.

I THOUGHT THE PHONE CALL TELLING ME FOWL WAS ALIVE WAS BAD NEWS.

LOOKS LIKE IT WAS GOOD NEWS IN DISGUISE.

SO YOU NAB THE FOWL KID THEN SQUEEZE HIM FOR THE CODE.

PROBLEM SOLVED, OR I'M NOT SPATZ ANTONELLI'S GOD-DAUGHTER.

YOU DON'T NEED TO SHOW OFF YOUR MOB CREDENTIALS TO ME, CARLA.

IT'S NOT QUITE THAT STRAIGHTFORWARD, THOUGH. THAT KID RUNS A TIGHT SHIP. FOWL MANOR IS LIKE A FORTRESS.

THIS IS A THIRTEEN-YEAR-OLD CHILD WE'RE TALKING ABOUT, RIGHT?

UM...WELL, HE'LL BE FOURTEEN IN A FEW MONTHS.

OH, THAT MAKES A BIG DIFFERENCE.

ANYWAY, ARNO IS INJURED. SOMEHOW FOWL BLEW HIS TEETH OUT.

OUCH.

IN FACT, THE KID INCAPACITATED ALL MY BEST PEOPLE. THE DENTAL PLAN ALONE IS GONNA COST ME A FORTUNE.

DOUBLE OUCH.

"I'm guessing I'm here because you want to contract the job to the Mob, right?"

"Exactly. But Ireland is an old-world kinda place. It's got to be just the right people. You got the right people, Carla?"

"Oh, I've got the perfect people...."

THE INKBLOT TATTOO PARLOUR, DOWNTOWN CHICAGO.

"The way I see it, you're going to need a metal man and a monkey. The metal man carries the gun, and monkey gets into hard-to-reach places."

"Your perfect metal man is Aloysius McGuire. Calls himself Loafers. Hails from Kilkenny, Ireland. His specialties are robbery and debt collection. Not bad for a guy five feet tall."

YOU LIKE THE SHOES, INKY?

YEAH. I LIKE 'EM. WHAT'RE THEY CALLED?

LOAFERS! LOAFERS, IDIOT. THEY'RE MY TRADEMARK.

OH, YEAH, LOAFERS. I FORGOT.

NOW THIS NEW TATTOO BETTER NOT HURT, INKY. OR YOU'LL BE HURTING SHORTLY AFTERWARDS.

BEEP BEEP

HELLO? THIS BETTER BE GOOD—OH, HELLO, MISS CARLA.

YEAH, SORRY.

WHAT, RIGHT NOW?

I'M GOING TO VISIT WHO?

BUT I DON'T HAVE AN UNCLE PATRICK.... OH, WAIT, I GET YA.

SO WHO'S THE MONKEY?

NEW GUY, JUST IN FROM L.A. MO DIGENCE. HE'S IRISH, LIKE YOU. AND HE'S SHORT LIKE YOU.

SHORT?!

SORRY, MISS FRAZETTI. IT'S JUST, I'VE HAD THE SHORT THING ALL MY LIFE.

WATCH YOUR TONE, McGUIRE.

SO? GET OVER IT. MY GODFATHER ALWAYS SAYS THERE'S NOTHING MORE DANGEROUS THAN A SHORT MAN WITH SOMETHING TO PROVE. THAT'S WHY YOU GOT THE JOB.

I SUPPOSE.

ANYWAY, COMPARED TO THIS MO, YOU'RE A REGULAR GIANT.

REALLY? WHAT EXACTLY IS THIS MO GUY LIKE, THEN?

HE'S... UNUSUAL.

MULCH DIGGUMS'S HIDEOUT, CHICAGO.

Dear Cousin Nord, I'm sorry to report that your old tunnel-dwarf buddy has fallen on hard times. A few months ago I was living it up in a Los Angeles penthouse with a million dollars in the bank. I should have known it wouldn't last.

Tragically, my money was frozen by a bunch of do-gooders called the Criminal Assets Bureau. I now find myself living in much-reduced circumstances, passing myself off as a human working for the Mob in ~~Chicago~~ a big city.

I can't tell you which city in case this falls into the wrong hands.

KNOCK KNOCK!

I'm still on the run for borrowing those bars of gold from the Holly Short ransom fund.

Some people have really long memories.

HURRY IT UP, MO. I'M GETTING OLD OUT HERE.

QUITE A LOOK YOU'VE GOT GOING HERE. MOULD AND WOODLICE. I LIKE IT.

OKAY, LISTEN UP, MO. I HAVE A SPECIAL JOB FOR YOU.

THE KIND OF JOB WHERE THERE'S A BIG PAYOFF IF YOU DO IT RIGHT?

NO, THE KIND OF JOB WHERE THERE'S A VERY PAINFUL PAYOFF IF YOU DO IT WRONG.

YOU GOT THIS ASSIGNMENT BECAUSE OF THE OUTSTANDING JOB YOU DID WITH THAT VAN GOGH. AND BECAUSE YOU HAVE AN IRISH PASSPORT. THAT'S WHERE YOU'RE GOING— TO IRELAND.

YEAH? WHO'S THE MUTT?

MUTT?!

YOU BETTA WATCH YOUR MOUTH, DIGENCE!

EASY, LOAFERS, WATCH YOUR TEMPER. THIS IS LOAFERS MCGUIRE, YOUR PARTNER. HE'S THE METAL MAN. IT'S A TWO-TIERED JOB.

YOU OPEN THE DOORS. LOAFERS ESCORTS THE MARK BACK HERE.

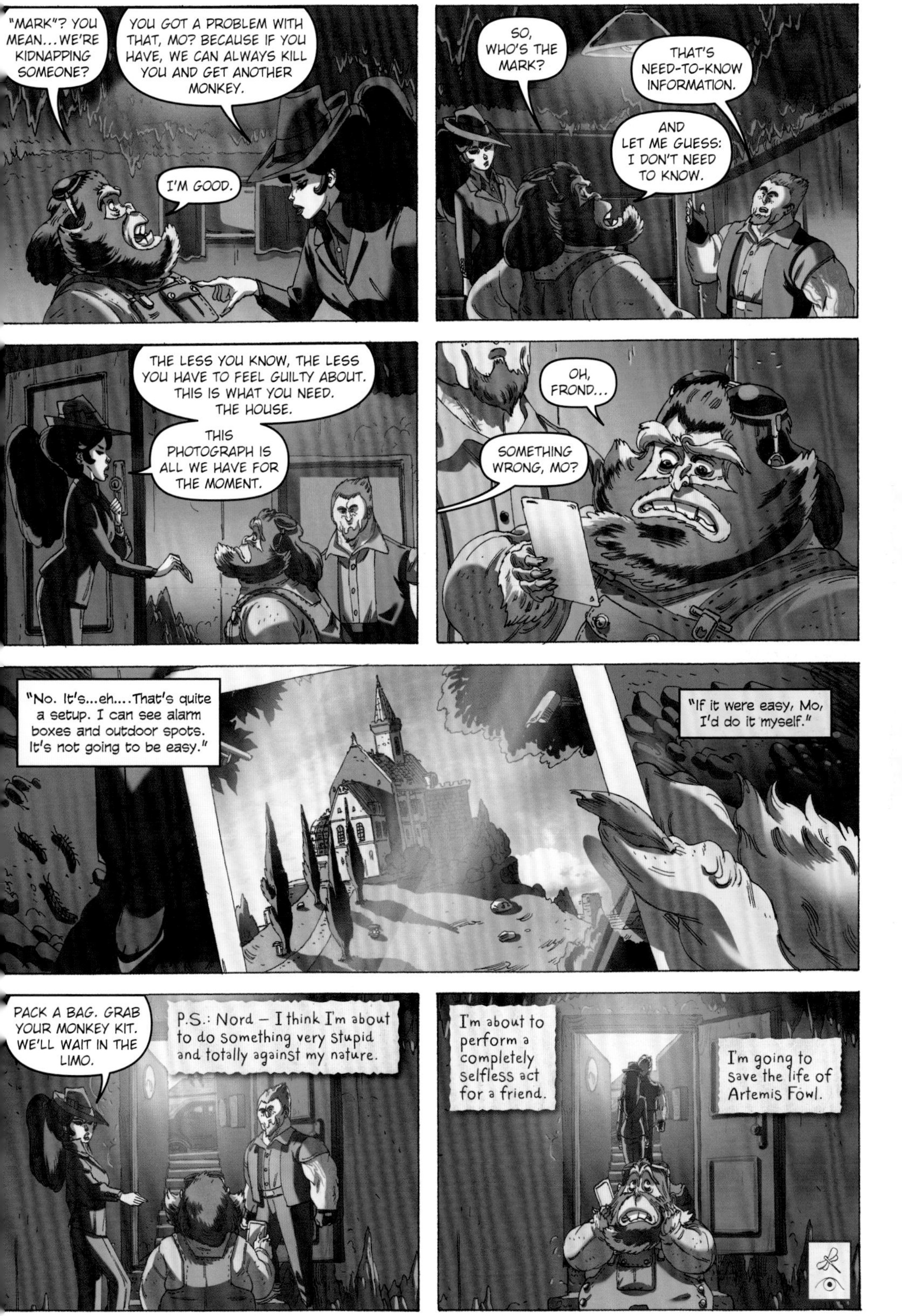
"MARK"? YOU MEAN... WE'RE KIDNAPPING SOMEONE?
YOU GOT A PROBLEM WITH THAT, MO? BECAUSE IF YOU HAVE, WE CAN ALWAYS KILL YOU AND GET ANOTHER MONKEY.
I'M GOOD.
SO, WHO'S THE MARK?
THAT'S NEED-TO-KNOW INFORMATION.
AND LET ME GUESS: I DON'T NEED TO KNOW.
THE LESS YOU KNOW, THE LESS YOU HAVE TO FEEL GUILTY ABOUT. THIS IS WHAT YOU NEED. THE HOUSE.
THIS PHOTOGRAPH IS ALL WE HAVE FOR THE MOMENT.
OH, FROND...
SOMETHING WRONG, MO?
"No. It's...eh....That's quite a setup. I can see alarm boxes and outdoor spots. It's not going to be easy."
"If it were easy, Mo, I'd do it myself."
PACK A BAG. GRAB YOUR MONKEY KIT. WE'LL WAIT IN THE LIMO.
P.S.: Nord – I think I'm about to do something very stupid and totally against my nature.
I'm about to perform a completely selfless act for a friend.
I'm going to save the life of Artemis Fowl.

My father lies in his hospital bed recovering.

His last words to me chase themselves around in my mind.

"Gold isn't all-important. We have everything we need right here. The three of us."

CHAPTER 6: ASSAULT ON FOWL MANOR

Was it possible that magic had transformed my father?

I had to know.

ME? YOU ARE THE PRIORITY HERE, FATHER.

I'VE BEEN EXPECTING YOU, ARTY. WE NEED TO TALK...ABOUT YOU.

PLEASE DON'T PLAY THE INNOCENT, ARTEMIS.

I'VE CALLED A FEW OF MY LAW-ENFORCEMENT CONTACTS.

APPARENTLY YOU HAVE BEEN ACTIVE IN MY ABSENCE. VERY ACTIVE.

Am I about to be scolded or praised?

NOT SO LONG AGO I WOULD HAVE BEEN VERY IMPRESSED. BUT NOW, SPEAKING AS A FATHER, THINGS HAVE TO CHANGE.

YOU MUST RECLAIM YOUR CHILDHOOD. AND YOU MUST RETURN TO SCHOOL.

BUT, FATHER!

I HAVE PROMISED YOUR MOTHER THAT THE FOWLS ARE ON THE STRAIGHT AND NARROW FROM NOW ON. *ALL* OF THE FOWLS.

I HAVE ANOTHER CHANCE, AND I WILL NOT WASTE IT ON GREED.

WE ARE A FAMILY NOW. A PROPER ONE.

AGREED, ARTEMIS?

AGREED.

I decide to proceed as planned with the Jon Spiro meeting. One last adventure. What could go wrong?

ARTEMIS?

ANYBODY HOME?

BUTLER! YOU'VE COME BACK TO US.

IT'S A SURPRISE TO ME. I NEVER EXPECTED TO SEE YOU, OR ANYONE, EVER AGAIN.

ARTEMIS, WHAT HAS HAPPENED? I SHOULDN'T BE ALIVE.

BLUNT SHOT YOU. IT WAS A FATAL WOUND, AND HOLLY WASN'T AROUND TO HELP, SO I FROZE YOU UNTIL SHE ARRIVED.

CRYOGENICS? ONLY ARTEMIS FOWL. YOU USED THE FISH FREEZERS, I SUPPOSE.

I TRUST I AM NOT PART FRESHWATER TROUT NOW?

THERE WERE... COMPLICATIONS.

COMPLICATIONS?

IT WAS A DIFFICULT HEALING. FOALY WARNED ME, BUT I INSISTED WE PRESS ON....

IT'S ALL RIGHT, ARTEMIS. I'M ALIVE.

ANYTHING IS BETTER THAN THE ALTERNATIVE.

"Prepare yourself and take a look, old friend."

"Just how long was I out??"

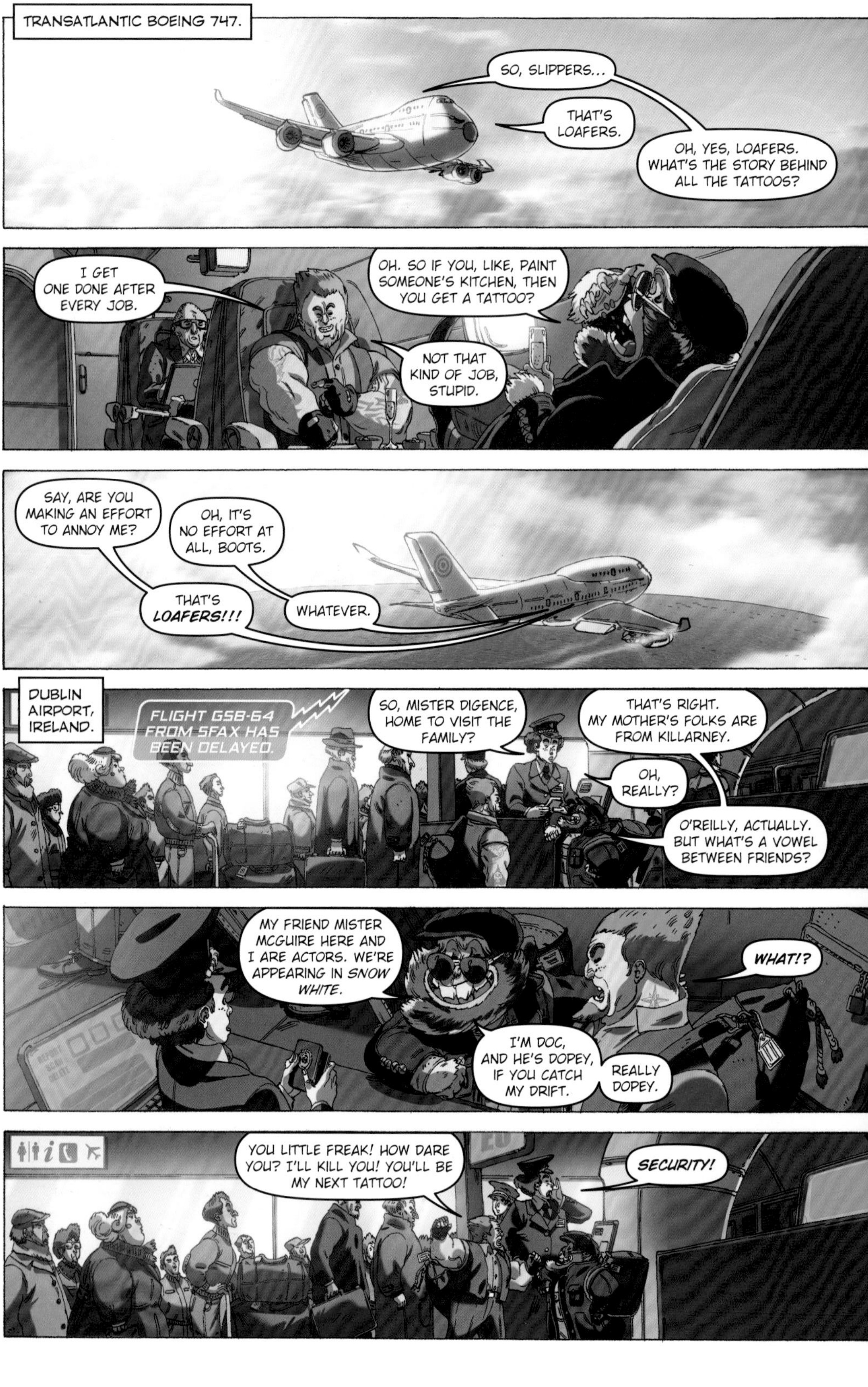

TRANSATLANTIC BOEING 747.
SO, SLIPPERS...
THAT'S LOAFERS.
OH, YES, LOAFERS. WHAT'S THE STORY BEHIND ALL THE TATTOOS?
I GET ONE DONE AFTER EVERY JOB.
OH. SO IF YOU, LIKE, PAINT SOMEONE'S KITCHEN, THEN YOU GET A TATTOO?
NOT THAT KIND OF JOB, STUPID.
SAY, ARE YOU MAKING AN EFFORT TO ANNOY ME?
OH, IT'S NO EFFORT AT ALL, BOOTS.
THAT'S LOAFERS!!!
WHATEVER.
DUBLIN AIRPORT, IRELAND.
FLIGHT GSB-64 FROM SFAX HAS BEEN DELAYED.
SO, MISTER DIGENCE, HOME TO VISIT THE FAMILY?
THAT'S RIGHT. MY MOTHER'S FOLKS ARE FROM KILLARNEY.
OH, REALLY?
O'REILLY, ACTUALLY. BUT WHAT'S A VOWEL BETWEEN FRIENDS?
MY FRIEND MISTER MCGUIRE HERE AND I ARE ACTORS. WE'RE APPEARING IN SNOW WHITE.
WHAT!?
I'M DOC, AND HE'S DOPEY, IF YOU CATCH MY DRIFT.
REALLY DOPEY.
YOU LITTLE FREAK! HOW DARE YOU? I'LL KILL YOU! YOU'LL BE MY NEXT TATTOO!
SECURITY!

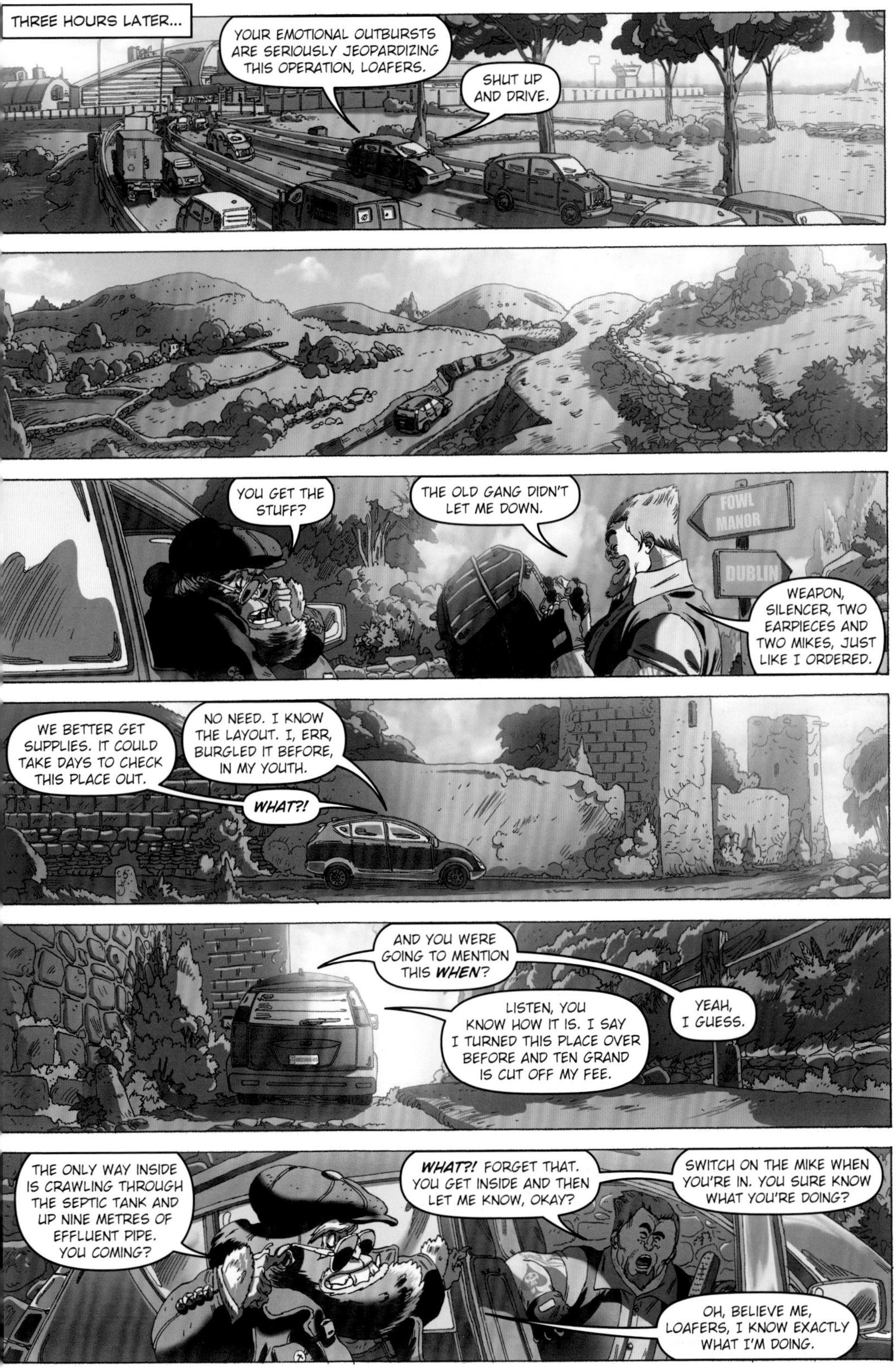
THREE HOURS LATER...
YOUR EMOTIONAL OUTBURSTS ARE SERIOUSLY JEOPARDIZING THIS OPERATION, LOAFERS.
SHUT UP AND DRIVE.
YOU GET THE STUFF?
THE OLD GANG DIDN'T LET ME DOWN.
FOWL MANOR
DUBLIN
WEAPON, SILENCER, TWO EARPIECES AND TWO MIKES, JUST LIKE I ORDERED.
WE BETTER GET SUPPLIES. IT COULD TAKE DAYS TO CHECK THIS PLACE OUT.
NO NEED. I KNOW THE LAYOUT. I, ERR, BURGLED IT BEFORE, IN MY YOUTH.
WHAT?!
AND YOU WERE GOING TO MENTION THIS *WHEN*?
YEAH, I GUESS.
LISTEN, YOU KNOW HOW IT IS. I SAY I TURNED THIS PLACE OVER BEFORE AND TEN GRAND IS CUT OFF MY FEE.
THE ONLY WAY INSIDE IS CRAWLING THROUGH THE SEPTIC TANK AND UP NINE METRES OF EFFLUENT PIPE. YOU COMING?
WHAT?! FORGET THAT. YOU GET INSIDE AND THEN LET ME KNOW, OKAY?
SWITCH ON THE MIKE WHEN YOU'RE IN. YOU SURE KNOW WHAT YOU'RE DOING?
OH, BELIEVE ME, LOAFERS, I KNOW EXACTLY WHAT I'M DOING.

Butler finishes clipping and shaving and begins to look like his old self again.

His older self.

EVERYTHING IS DIFFERENT, ARTEMIS. I CAN'T GUARD YOU ANY MORE.

SOON I WON'T NEED GUARDING. HOLLY WAS RIGHT.

MY GRAND SCHEMES GENERALLY LEAD TO PEOPLE GETTING HURT.

AS SOON AS WE HAVE DEALT WITH SPIRO, I INTEND TO CONCENTRATE ON MY EDUCATION.

YOU MAKE DEALING WITH SPIRO SOUND LIKE A FOREGONE CONCLUSION.

JON SPIRO IS A DANGEROUS MAN, ARTEMIS.

I THOUGHT YOU WOULD HAVE LEARNED THAT.

I HAVE, OLD FRIEND. BELIEVE ME, I WON'T UNDERESTIMATE HIM AGAIN. I HAVE ALREADY BEGUN TO FORMULATE A PLAN, PROVIDING HOLLY AGREES TO HELP.

WHERE IS HOLLY, ANYWAY? I NEED TO THANK HER. AGAIN.

"She has gone to complete the Ritual.

"I'm sure you can guess where."

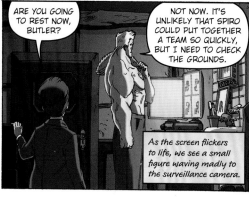

ARE YOU GOING TO REST NOW, BUTLER?

NOT NOW. IT'S UNLIKELY THAT SPIRO COULD PUT TOGETHER A TEAM SO QUICKLY, BUT I NEED TO CHECK THE GROUNDS.

As the screen flickers to life, we see a small figure waving madly to the surveillance camera.

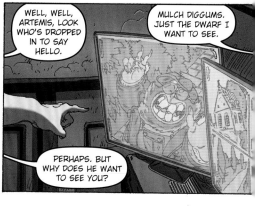

WELL, WELL, ARTEMIS, LOOK WHO'S DROPPED IN TO SAY HELLO.

MULCH DIGGUMS. JUST THE DWARF I WANT TO SEE.

PERHAPS. BUT WHY DOES HE WANT TO SEE YOU?

Mulch is as melodramatic as always and insists on food before he'll explain anything.

SO, MUD BOY, THAT'S YOUR IDEA OF MAKING A SANDWICH?

IT'S MORE DIFFICULT THAN IT LOOKS.

Mulch cranks open his massive jaws, and the whole thing disappears in one gulp.

NEXT TIME, MORE MUSTARD.

He brushes the crumbs from his shirt and starts talking.

NOT THE BEST-CONSTRUCTED SNACK I'VE EVER EATEN, BUT TASTY ANYWAY.

HEY, MULCH HAS TURNED ON HIS MICROPHONE. WHO'S HE GABBING TO?

ANYWAY, YOU SHOULD BE THANKING ME, MUD BOY. I'VE CAME ALL THE WAY FROM CHICAGO TO SAVE YOUR LIFE.

SURELY THAT'S WORTH ONE LOUSY SANDWICH?

WHAT?! WHY, YOU LITTLE BACKSTABBING FREAK!! YOU'RE A WALKING DEAD MAN!

Mulch starts talking and doesn't stop. Not even for breath.

HMMM... JON SPIRO IS PROBABLY PULLING THE STRINGS. BUT I WORK DIRECTLY FOR THE ANTONELLI FAMILY.

OF COURSE, THEY'VE NO IDEA I'M A TUNNEL DWARF.

THEY JUST THINK I'M THE BEST CAT BURGLAR IN THE BUSINESS.

Butler calls up the external camera views.

LET'S SEE WHERE THIS PARTNER OF YOURS IS, THEN, MULCH.

GLAD TO SEE YOU'RE ALIVE, BY THE WAY, BIG MAN. THERE WAS A RUMOUR GOING AROUND THE UNDERWORLD THAT YOU WERE DEAD.

I WAS. BUT I'M BETTER NOW. OH...

YEAH?

MAYBE NOT FOR LONG.

Oh no.

To be fair, Mulch recovers well.

I THOUGHT I TOLD YOU TO WAIT OUTSIDE.

YOU DID. BUT THAT WAS BEFORE YOU ACCIDENTALLY SWITCHED YOUR MIKE ON, MO. OR SHOULD I SAY MULCH?

I'M IN, SO I GUESS I DON'T NEED A MONKEY ANY MORE, DO I?

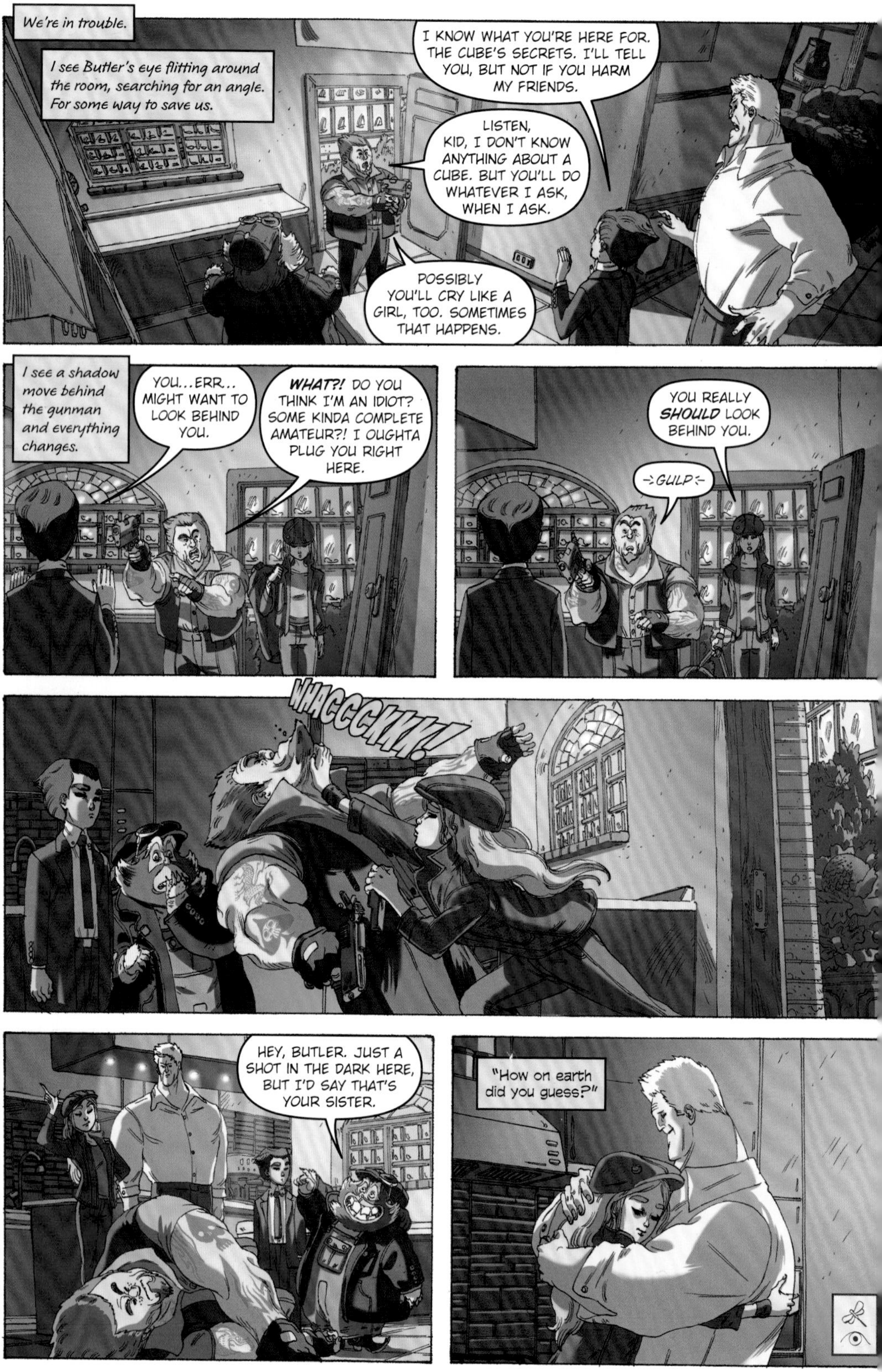

We're in trouble.
I see Butler's eye flitting around the room, searching for an angle. For some way to save us.
I KNOW WHAT YOU'RE HERE FOR. THE CUBE'S SECRETS. I'LL TELL YOU, BUT NOT IF YOU HARM MY FRIENDS.
LISTEN, KID, I DON'T KNOW ANYTHING ABOUT A CUBE. BUT YOU'LL DO WHATEVER I ASK, WHEN I ASK.
POSSIBLY YOU'LL CRY LIKE A GIRL, TOO. SOMETIMES THAT HAPPENS.
I see a shadow move behind the gunman and everything changes.
YOU...ERR... MIGHT WANT TO LOOK BEHIND YOU.
WHAT?! DO YOU THINK I'M AN IDIOT? SOME KINDA COMPLETE AMATEUR?! I OUGHTA PLUG YOU RIGHT HERE.
YOU REALLY SHOULD LOOK BEHIND YOU.
GULP
WHACCCKKK!
HEY, BUTLER. JUST A SHOT IN THE DARK HERE, BUT I'D SAY THAT'S YOUR SISTER.
"How on earth did you guess?"

Somehow it feels like old times....

LOOKS LIKE THE GANG'S ALL HERE.

CHAPTER 7: BEST-LAID PLANS

Even if Commander Root isn't happy about it. Or Holly's report.

PERSONAL REPORT: CAPTAIN HOLLY SHORT
Yesterday I responded to an alert from the Sentinel warning system. The call was made by Artemis Fowl, a Mud Man known to the LEP. His associate Butler had been mortally injured in a shooting and he requested my assistance with a healing.

So I'm hoping you're going to tell me you refused, and performed a mind wipe as per regulations?

NO. TAKING INTO ACCOUNT BUTLER'S HELP DURING THE GOBLIN REBELLION, I PERFORMED THE HEALING AND BROUGHT HIM BACK.

What?!

Much to his own annoyance, Mulch had been attempting to weasel a reward from me when Holly returned.

I'M TRYING TO HELP. I REALLY SHOULDN'T BE CUFFED TO A CHAIR.

YOU'D RATHER BE CUFFED TO A TABLE?

YOU'RE MISSING MY POINT.

Tell the convict to shut up! Do you know how many rules we're breaking just having this conversation, Holly?

Okay, so if Fowl was responsible for the probe, is the alert now over?

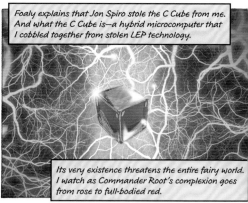

Foaly explains that Jon Spiro stole the C Cube from me. And what the C Cube is—a hybrid microcomputer that I cobbled together from stolen LEP technology.

Its very existence threatens the entire fairy world. I watch as Commander Root's complexion goes from rose to full-bodied red.

You have thirty seconds, Artemis. Sell it to me. Why should I let Holly help you?

If I get this wrong, then Holly and Mulch are on the next shuttle heading home. And my chances of beating Spiro disappear with them.

SPIRO HAS FAIRY TECHNOLOGY.

IT'S UNLIKELY HE'LL BE ABLE TO USE IT IN THE SHORT TERM.

BUT IT WILL POINT HIS SCIENTISTS TOWARDS ION TECHNOLOGY.

THE MAN'S A MEGALOMANIAC, WITH NO RESPECT FOR LIFE OR THE ENVIRONMENT.

SOONER OR LATER, THE C CUBE WILL LEAD HIM TO HAVEN CITY, AND WHEN THAT HAPPENS, ALL LIFE ON EARTH IS AT RISK.

GIVE ME HOLLY AND MULCH AND I CAN CLEAR UP THIS MESS.

Your mess.

YES... *MY* MESS.

Commander Root confers with Foaly.

THIS DOESN'T LOOK GOOD.

Listen up, Fowl, here's the deal.

It's a take-it-or-leave-it offer.

This is serious. We cannot afford to risk that this Spiro individual will activate another probe and discover Haven City.

It would be the end of everything.

I'm going to put together an insertion team of LEP's finest officers. A fully tooled-up Retrieval team.

IN AN URBAN AREA? COMMANDER, THAT COULD TURN INTO A *DISASTER*. PLEASE, LET ME TAKE A CRACK AT IT.

As I was about to say...it will take me forty-eight hours to clear the operation, so you have until then to do what you can.

YOU'LL COVER FOR US?

Yes.

I can't let you have Foaly. But Diggums can help if he wants. It's his choice.

I might even drop a couple of the burglary charges. But he still does time for the bullion robbery.

GIVE ME A BREAK, JULIUS. EVERY TIME THERE'S A FOWL SITUATION, IT'S ME THAT SAVES YOUR BACON.

I'M SURE WHATEVER PLAN ARTEMIS CONCOCTS WILL FEATURE YOURS TRULY.

MOST PROBABLY IN SOME RIDICULOUSLY DANGEROUS CAPACITY.

That's the best I can do. If you fail, then the Retrieval team is waiting in the wings.

I UNDERSTAND. THANK YOU.

There is a condition.

I know what's coming next.

YOU WANT A MIND WIPE, CORRECT?

That's right, Artemis. You are a severe liability to the People. If we help you, then you and your staff would have to submit to mind wipes.

AND IF I DON'T AGREE?

We go straight to plan B, and you get wiped anyway.

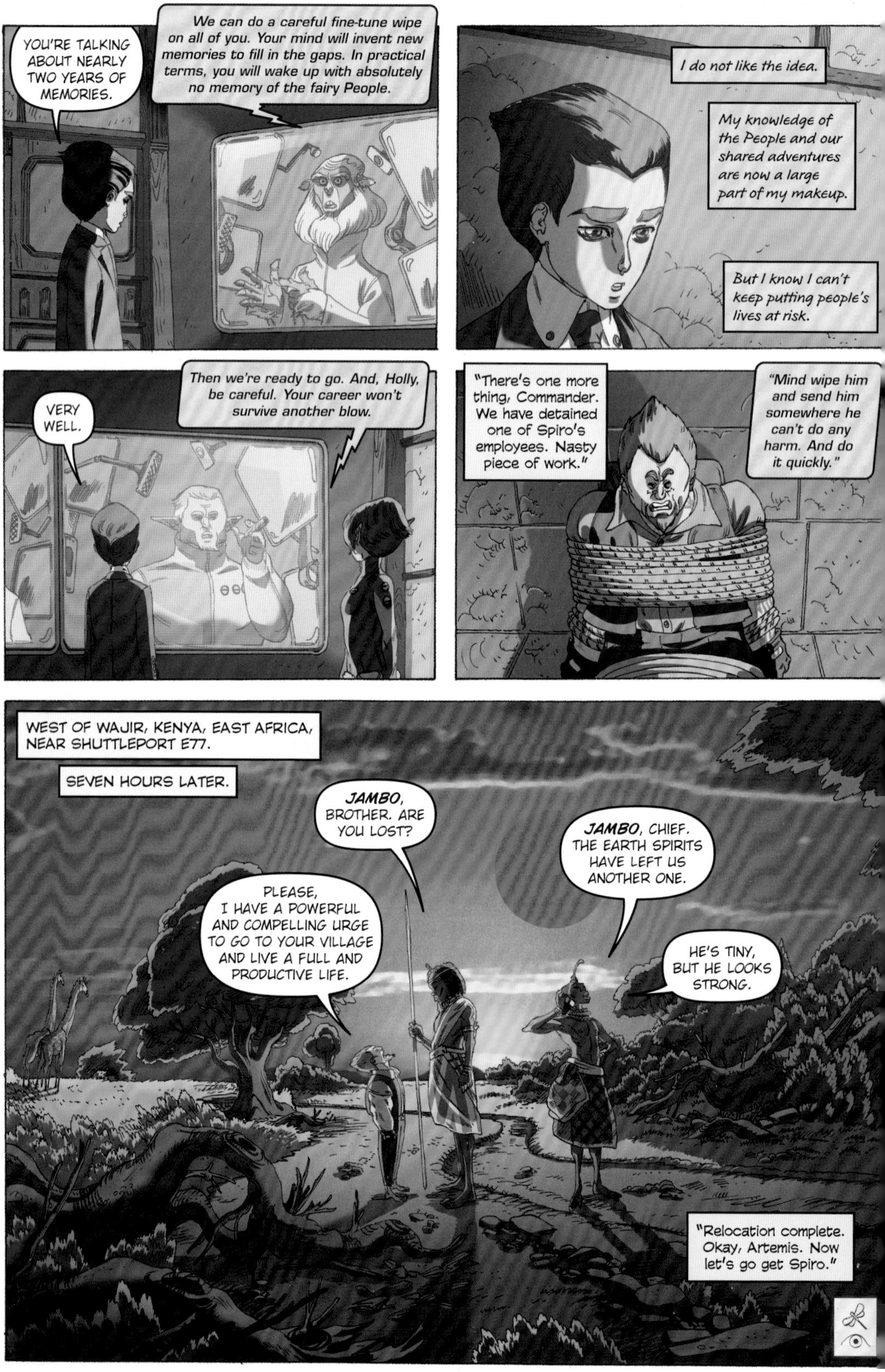
YOU'RE TALKING ABOUT NEARLY TWO YEARS OF MEMORIES.
We can do a careful fine-tune wipe on all of you. Your mind will invent new memories to fill in the gaps. In practical terms, you will wake up with absolutely no memory of the fairy People.
I do not like the idea.
My knowledge of the People and our shared adventures are now a large part of my makeup.
But I know I can't keep putting people's lives at risk.
VERY WELL.
Then we're ready to go. And, Holly, be careful. Your career won't survive another blow.
"There's one more thing, Commander. We have detained one of Spiro's employees. Nasty piece of work."
"Mind wipe him and send him somewhere he can't do any harm. And do it quickly."
WEST OF WAJIR, KENYA, EAST AFRICA, NEAR SHUTTLEPORT E77.
SEVEN HOURS LATER.
JAMBO, BROTHER. ARE YOU LOST?
PLEASE, I HAVE A POWERFUL AND COMPELLING URGE TO GO TO YOUR VILLAGE AND LIVE A FULL AND PRODUCTIVE LIFE.
JAMBO, CHIEF. THE EARTH SPIRITS HAVE LEFT US ANOTHER ONE.
HE'S TINY, BUT HE LOOKS STRONG.
"Relocation complete. Okay, Artemis. Now let's go get Spiro."

EXCERPT FROM ARTEMIS FOWL'S DIARY. DISK 2. ENCRYPTED.

Today, Father was fitted for his prosthetic limb.

He joked throughout the entire process, as though he were being fitted for a new suit on Grafton Street.

This "new man" who is my father.

CHAPTER 8:
HOOKS, LINES AND SINKERS

I find myself making excuses just to be with him and enjoy his presence.

SHALL I TELL YOU SOMETHING, ARTY?

I'VE BEEN THINKING ABOUT MY LIFE, HOW I WASTED IT GATHERING RICHES, WHATEVER THE COST TO MY FAMILY.

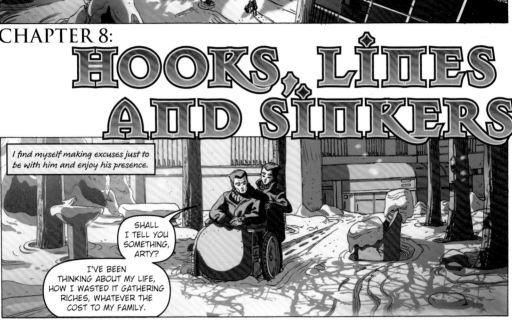

IN A MAN'S LIFE, HE GETS FEW CHANCES TO MAKE A DIFFERENCE. TO DO THE RIGHT THING. TO BE A HERO, IF YOU WILL. I INTEND TO BECOME INVOLVED IN THAT STRUGGLE.

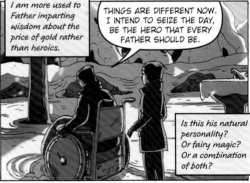

I am more used to Father imparting wisdom about the price of gold rather than heroics.

THINGS ARE DIFFERENT NOW. I INTEND TO SEIZE THE DAY, BE THE HERO THAT EVERY FATHER SHOULD BE.

Is this his natural personality? Or fairy magic? Or a combination of both?

WHAT ABOUT YOU, ARTY? WILL YOU MAKE THE JOURNEY WITH ME? WILL YOU TAKE YOUR CHANCE TO BE A HERO?

I don't respond.

I don't know the answer.

FOWL MANOR. NOW.

I need a plan.

I need a plan that is completely and utterly foolproof.

I meditate.

For hours.

Speaking into a voice-activated digital recorder when ideas hit.

Nothing must interrupt this.

I put the plan—in parts—on to computer CDs.

PLEASE STUDY THESE. THEY CONTAIN DETAILS OF YOUR ASSIGNMENTS. NONE OF YOU HAS THE WHOLE PLAN.

AFTER YOU'VE MEMORIZED THE CONTENTS, PLEASE DESTROY THE DISKS.

A CD. HOW QUAINT. IN HAVEN CITY WE HAVE THOSE IN MUSEUMS.

NOTHING FOR ME, ARTEMIS?

I wait until the others have gone and take Butler aside.

I'M NOT GOING WITH YOU, AM I?

NO, OLD FRIEND. I HAVE A VITAL TASK FOR YOU HERE.

IT CONCERNS THE MIND WIPES. WE MUST ENSURE THAT SOMETHING SURVIVES FOALY'S SEARCH. SOMETHING THAT WILL TRIGGER OUR MEMORIES OF THE PEOPLE.

I outline the false email and computer trails I plan to use to throw Foaly off the scent.

NO DOUBT WE WILL BE MESMERIZED AND QUESTIONED. IN THE PAST WE HAVE HIDDEN FROM THE *MESMER* BEHIND MIRRORED SUNGLASSES.

BUT FOR THIS WE NEED SOMETHING ELSE. HERE ARE THE BLUEPRINTS...

IT'S POSSIBLE. I KNOW SOMEONE IN LIMERICK WHO DOES THIS KIND OF WORK. I'LL VISIT HIM TOMORROW.

"Excellent. After that, you need to put everything we have on the People on disk. All documents, videos, schematics. Everything. Especially my diary."

"And where do we hide this disk?"

"I'd say this was about the same size as this, wouldn't you?"

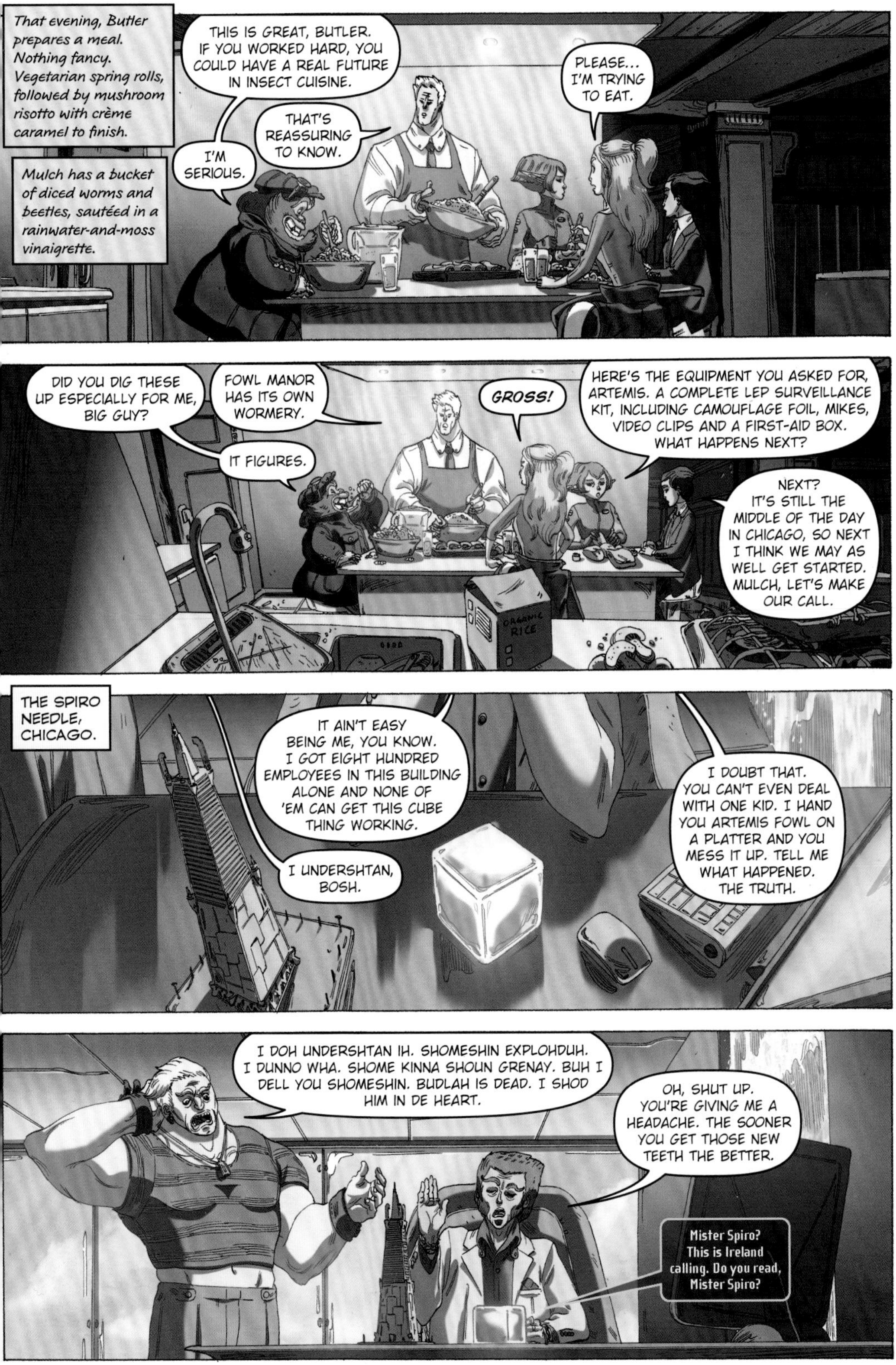
That evening, Butler prepares a meal. Nothing fancy. Vegetarian spring rolls, followed by mushroom risotto with crème caramel to finish.
Mulch has a bucket of diced worms and beetles, sautéed in a rainwater-and-moss vinaigrette.
THIS IS GREAT, BUTLER. IF YOU WORKED HARD, YOU COULD HAVE A REAL FUTURE IN INSECT CUISINE.
THAT'S REASSURING TO KNOW.
I'M SERIOUS.
PLEASE... I'M TRYING TO EAT.
DID YOU DIG THESE UP ESPECIALLY FOR ME, BIG GUY?
FOWL MANOR HAS ITS OWN WORMERY.
IT FIGURES.
GROSS!
HERE'S THE EQUIPMENT YOU ASKED FOR, ARTEMIS. A COMPLETE LEP SURVEILLANCE KIT, INCLUDING CAMOUFLAGE FOIL, MIKES, VIDEO CLIPS AND A FIRST-AID BOX. WHAT HAPPENS NEXT?
NEXT? IT'S STILL THE MIDDLE OF THE DAY IN CHICAGO, SO NEXT I THINK WE MAY AS WELL GET STARTED. MULCH, LET'S MAKE OUR CALL.
ORGANIC RICE
THE SPIRO NEEDLE, CHICAGO.
IT AIN'T EASY BEING ME, YOU KNOW. I GOT EIGHT HUNDRED EMPLOYEES IN THIS BUILDING ALONE AND NONE OF 'EM CAN GET THIS CUBE THING WORKING.
I UNDERSHTAN, BOSH.
I DOUBT THAT. YOU CAN'T EVEN DEAL WITH ONE KID. I HAND YOU ARTEMIS FOWL ON A PLATTER AND YOU MESS IT UP. TELL ME WHAT HAPPENED. THE TRUTH.
I DOH UNDERSHTAN IH. SHOMESHIN EXPLOHDUH. I DUNNO WHA. SHOME KINNA SHOUN GRENAY. BUH I DELL YOU SHOMESHIN. BUDLAH IS DEAD. I SHOD HIM IN DE HEART.
OH, SHUT UP. YOU'RE GIVING ME A HEADACHE. THE SOONER YOU GET THOSE NEW TEETH THE BETTER.
Mister Spiro? This is Ireland calling. Do you read, Mister Spiro?

HOW DID YOU GET THIS BOX WORKING?

MY NAME IS MO DIGENCE. I'M THE MONKEY FROM CARLA FRAZETTI'S TEAM.

I DON'T KNOW WHAT KIND OF BOX YOU HAVE AT YOUR END; I JUST HAVE A PLAIN OLD TELEPHONE AND A LITTLE KID WHO'S GOT YOUR NUMBER.

I can't see Spiro's face, but I'm guessing he's wearing a big smile as Mulch spins his tale.

The story goes like this: Loafers goes crazy and starts waving his gun about. Mulch thinks it's the wrong thing to do and stops him. Forcibly. Poor little Artemis gets so scared he tells Mulch everything.

YOU DID THE RIGHT THING, DIGENCE. NOW PUT THE FOWL KID ON.

NOT TOO COCKY NOW, EH, KID? LIKE I TOLD YOU, YOU DON'T HAVE THE GUTS FOR THIS JOB. YOU'RE GOING TO GET THIS CUBE WORKING FOR ME OR I'LL LET MO LOOSE ON YOU. GOT IT?

OF COURSE, MISTER SPIRO. I'D HAVE TO HAVE THE CUBE IN FRONT OF ME TO DO THAT, SO IF YOU'D JUST BRING IT OVER TO...

HOW STUPID DO YOU THINK I AM, FOWL?!

MO WILL BRING YOU TO THE SPIRO NEEDLE AND YOU'LL DISABLE THE ETERNITY CODE IN MY LAB RIGHT HERE, UNDER MY NOSE.

I DON'T SUPPOSE I HAVE A CHOICE.

YOU DON'T, KID, BUT DO THIS RIGHT AND I MIGHT JUST LET YOU GO. NOW FUEL UP YOUR LEARJET AND GET OVER HERE.

YOU GET THAT, DIGENCE? I'M COUNTING ON YOU TO GET THE KID TO CHICAGO. NOW MOVE.

=CLICK=

"I don't care what the doctors say, I think I'm going to celebrate with a cup of real coffee. Full caffeine, too.

"For a supposed genius, that kid sure is gullible. 'Do this right and I might just let you go.' He fell for that one hook, line and sinker."

"Yesh, Mishduh Shpiro. Hoo, line an' shinkuh."

DUBLIN AIRPORT.

Butler drives. Holly and Mulch huddle in the back, glad for the tinted glass.

OF COURSE, IT'S AGAINST PROTOCOL FOR YOU TO HAVE ARTEMIS AS YOUR PRINCIPAL. HE ALREADY KNOWS YOUR FIRST NAME, AND TRUTH BE TOLD, I THINK HE'S A LITTLE FOND OF YOU.

THIS IS JUST TEMPORARY. ACCORDING TO MADAME KO, I'M NOT READY TO BE ANYONE'S BODYGUARD JUST YET.

IF THIS MISSION WEREN'T SO VITAL TO HUMANS AND FAIRIES, I WOULDN'T LET YOU GO AT ALL.

I KNOW. I WILL BE CAREFUL. I PROMISE.

WITHOUT YOU BY MY SIDE, OLD FRIEND, I'LL FEEL AS THOUGH ONE OF MY LIMBS IS MISSING.

JULIET WILL KEEP YOU SAFE. I KNOW SHE WILL.

I'LL BE FINE. TRUST ME. I'M A GENIUS.

Juliet pilots the Learjet and I can't help being a little impressed.

YOU'VE GROWN UP A LOT IN TWO YEARS. LAST TIME I SAW YOU, YOU WERE A LITTLE GIRL.

A LOT CAN HAPPEN IN TWO YEARS. I SPENT MOST OF THAT TIME WRESTLING BIG HAIRY MEN.

YEAH, YOU SHOULD SEE FAIRY WRESTLING. TWO PUMPED-UP GNOMES HAVING IT OUT IN A ZERO-G CHAMBER. I'LL SEND YOU A VIDEODISC.

NO, YOU WON'T.

I remember the mind wipes.

"You're right. No, I won't."

Mulch enjoys reliving his glory days.

REMEMBER THAT TIME I NEARLY BLEW BUTLER'S HEAD OFF WITH A BLAST OF GAS? TRUTH IS, I DIDN'T EVEN REALIZE HE WAS THERE. I WAS JUST A LITTLE NERVOUS.

THAT MAKES ME FEEL BETTER.

A FLAWLESS PLAN SCUPPERED BY A BOWEL PROBLEM.

WE'D BETTER GET YOU KITTED OUT, ARTEMIS. WE'LL BE LANDING SOONER THAN YOU THINK.

GOOD IDEA. WHAT DO WE NEED NOW? THE THROAT MIKE AND AN IRIS-CAM?

LEP technology. the most advanced under the earth.

The throat mike is hidden under a memory latex that turns the colour of my skin. Completely undetectable.

IT'LL PICK UP WHATEVER IS SAID WITHIN A TEN-METRE RADIUS.

WE CAN'T RISK AN EARPIECE, SO WE CAN HEAR YOU BUT YOU WON'T BE ABLE TO HEAR US.

Holly produces the iris-cam.

THIS THING IS A MARVEL.

HI-RES RECORDABLE PICTURE WITH SEVERAL FILTER OPTIONS INCLUDING MAGNIFICATION AND THERMAL.

HEY, HOLLY, YOU'RE STARTING TO SOUND LIKE THAT BRAIN-BOX FOALY.

HOLLY, THIS LENS IS HAZEL.

OF COURSE. MY EYES ARE HAZEL.

I'M GLAD TO HEAR IT, HOLLY, BUT MINE AREN'T. MY EYES ARE BLUE. THIS ISN'T GOING TO WORK.

DON'T LOOK AT ME LIKE THAT, MUD BOY. YOU'RE THE GENIUS.

I CAN'T GO IN THERE WITH ONE HAZEL EYE AND ONE BLUE EYE. SPIRO WILL NOTICE.

WELL, YOU SHOULD HAVE THOUGHT OF THAT WHILE YOU WERE MEDITATING.

IT'S A LITTLE LATE NOW.

YOU'RE RIGHT, OF COURSE. THINKING IS MY RESPONSIBILITY, NOT YOURS.

HEY, WAS THAT AN INSULT?

I HAVE TO TELL YOU, ARTY, A SCREWUP THIS EARLY IN THE PROCEEDINGS DOESN'T EXACTLY FILL ME WITH CONFIDENCE.

"Very well, we will have to risk the hazel iris-cam. With any luck, Spiro won't notice it. And if he does, I can invent some excuse."

"It's your decision, Artemis. I just hope you haven't finally met your match."

"Well, I guess we're all about to find out."

Spiro is waiting for us at the airport. Just in time, I remember I'm supposed to be a terrified kid.

MOVE IT, KID. WE DON'T WANT TO KEEP MISTER SPIRO WAITING.

I have to be humble, too. Not easy.

Spiro is not impressed.

NICE ACTING, SONNY. BUT PARDON ME IF I DOUBT THE GREAT ARTEMIS FOWL HAS FALLEN APART QUITE SO EASILY. ARNO, CHECK THE PLANE.

YES, BOSS.

Blunt and his new set of teeth check the plane.

All he finds is an innocent flight attendant straightening the headrest covers. Holly hides in an overhead locker.

OH, THERE'S NO ONE ELSE ON BOARD.

MASTER ARTEMIS FLIES THE PLANE HIMSELF.

YOU BIT OFF MORE THAN YOU COULD CHEW WHEN YOU AGREED TO COME HERE, KID. THE SPIRO NEEDLE HAS THE BEST SECURITY ON THE PLANET.

WE'VE GOT STUFF IN THERE THAT EVEN THE MILITARY DON'T HAVE.

Spiro might have stuff that the military doesn't have, but we've got stuff that humans have never seen. This is going to be interesting.

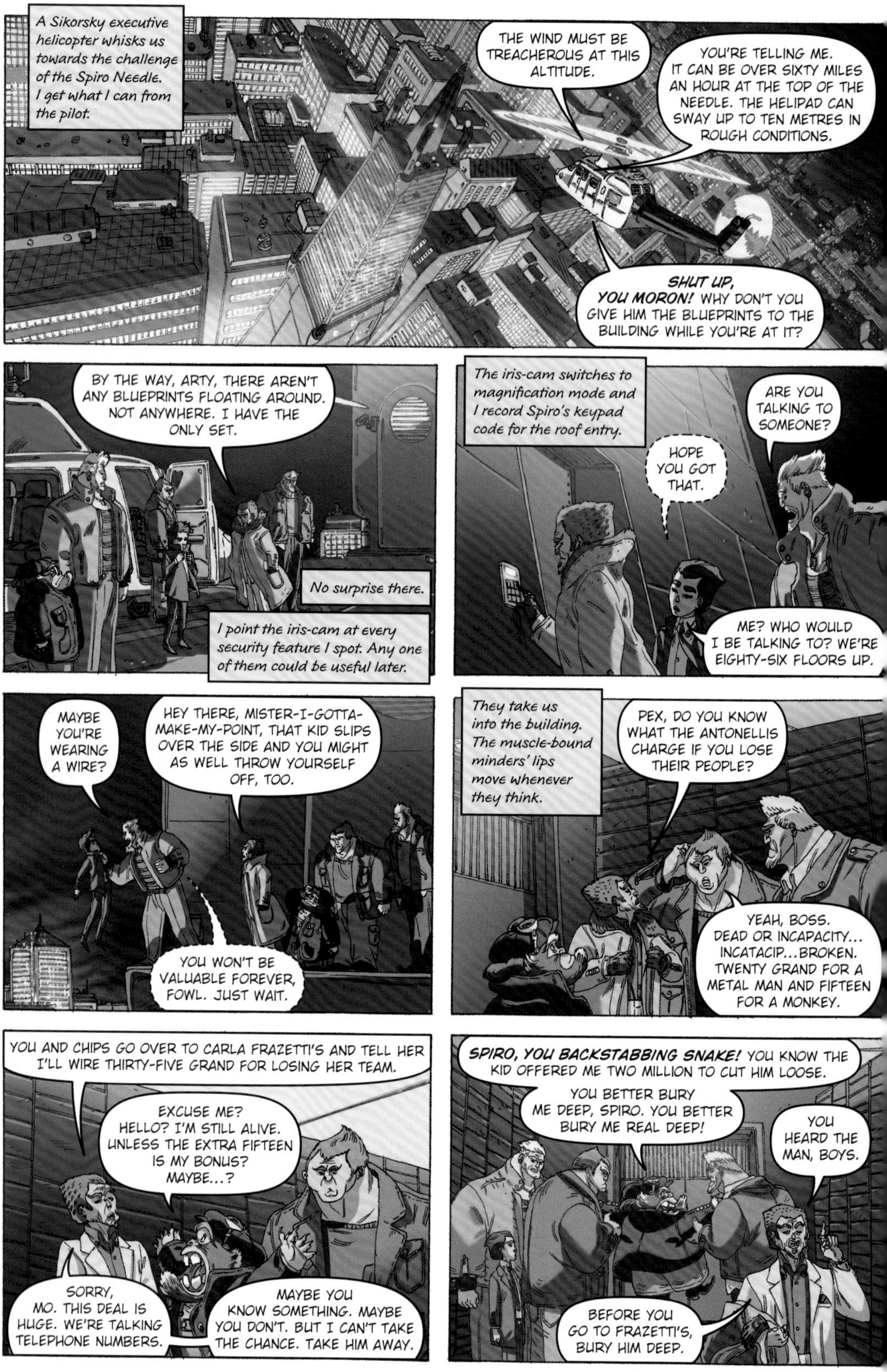
A Sikorsky executive helicopter whisks us towards the challenge of the Spiro Needle. I get what I can from the pilot.
THE WIND MUST BE TREACHEROUS AT THIS ALTITUDE.
YOU'RE TELLING ME. IT CAN BE OVER SIXTY MILES AN HOUR AT THE TOP OF THE NEEDLE. THE HELIPAD CAN SWAY UP TO TEN METRES IN ROUGH CONDITIONS.
SHUT UP, YOU MORON! WHY DON'T YOU GIVE HIM THE BLUEPRINTS TO THE BUILDING WHILE YOU'RE AT IT?
BY THE WAY, ARTY, THERE AREN'T ANY BLUEPRINTS FLOATING AROUND. NOT ANYWHERE. I HAVE THE ONLY SET.
No surprise there.
I point the iris-cam at every security feature I spot. Any one of them could be useful later.
The iris-cam switches to magnification mode and I record Spiro's keypad code for the roof entry.
ARE YOU TALKING TO SOMEONE?
HOPE YOU GOT THAT.
ME? WHO WOULD I BE TALKING TO? WE'RE EIGHTY-SIX FLOORS UP.
MAYBE YOU'RE WEARING A WIRE?
HEY THERE, MISTER-I-GOTTA-MAKE-MY-POINT, THAT KID SLIPS OVER THE SIDE AND YOU MIGHT AS WELL THROW YOURSELF OFF, TOO.
YOU WON'T BE VALUABLE FOREVER, FOWL. JUST WAIT.
They take us into the building. The muscle-bound minders' lips move whenever they think.
PEX, DO YOU KNOW WHAT THE ANTONELLIS CHARGE IF YOU LOSE THEIR PEOPLE?
YEAH, BOSS. DEAD OR INCAPACITY... INCATACIP...BROKEN. TWENTY GRAND FOR A METAL MAN AND FIFTEEN FOR A MONKEY.
YOU AND CHIPS GO OVER TO CARLA FRAZETTI'S AND TELL HER I'LL WIRE THIRTY-FIVE GRAND FOR LOSING HER TEAM.
EXCUSE ME? HELLO? I'M STILL ALIVE. UNLESS THE EXTRA FIFTEEN IS MY BONUS? MAYBE...?
SORRY, MO. THIS DEAL IS HUGE. WE'RE TALKING TELEPHONE NUMBERS.
MAYBE YOU KNOW SOMETHING. MAYBE YOU DON'T. BUT I CAN'T TAKE THE CHANCE. TAKE HIM AWAY.
SPIRO, YOU BACKSTABBING SNAKE! YOU KNOW THE KID OFFERED ME TWO MILLION TO CUT HIM LOOSE.
YOU BETTER BURY ME DEEP, SPIRO. YOU BETTER BURY ME REAL DEEP!
YOU HEARD THE MAN, BOYS.
BEFORE YOU GO TO FRAZETTI'S, BURY HIM DEEP.

Mulch is dragged away. Spiro leads me down towards the vault room where Dr. Pearson greets us.

WE WOULDN'T WANT ANY BUGS IN HERE. ESPECIALLY NOT THE ELECTRONIC KIND.

THIS SCANNER INCLUDES THERMAL, X-RAY AND METAL-DETECTION BEAMS, SO *NOTHING* GETS THROUGH HERE. ONE OF MY OWN INVENTIONS.

I hold my breath and pray that Foaly's equipment is as good as he thinks it is.

AHA. WHAT HAVE WE HERE?

VERY CLEVER. A MICRO-BUG HIDDEN INSIDE A JACKET BUTTON. OUR YOUNG FRIEND WAS ATTEMPTING TO SPY ON US, MISTER SPIRO.

Spiro's not angry. He just gloats.

YOU SEE, KID? YOU MAY BE SOME KIND OF GENIUS, BUT SURVEILLANCE AND ESPIONAGE ARE MY BUSINESS. YOU CAN'T SLIP ANYTHING PAST ME.

YOU GET IT?

The decoy works. Pearson was smart, but Foaly was smarter.

UMMM, THE TITANIUM DOORS MIGHT BE A BIT OVERKILL, DON'T YOU THINK?

YOU NEVER KNOW. SOME CROOKED BUSINESSMAN MIGHT ATTEMPT TO RELIEVE ME OF MY PRIZE.

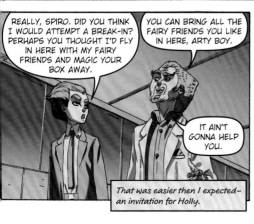

REALLY, SPIRO. DID YOU THINK I WOULD ATTEMPT A BREAK-IN? PERHAPS YOU THOUGHT I'D FLY IN HERE WITH MY FAIRY FRIENDS AND MAGIC MY BOX AWAY.

YOU CAN BRING ALL THE FAIRY FRIENDS YOU LIKE IN HERE, ARTY BOY.

IT AIN'T GONNA HELP YOU.

That was easier then I expected– an invitation for Holly.

EVEN IF YOU COULD GET PAST THE LOCKED DOORS, SENSOR PADS AND DOOR CODES, COULD YOU DO THIS?

JON SPIRO. I AM THE BOSS, SO OPEN UP QUICK.

Three things happen very quickly.

A laser scans his eye, a print plate takes his left thumbprint and then Spiro speaks into a voice analyser.

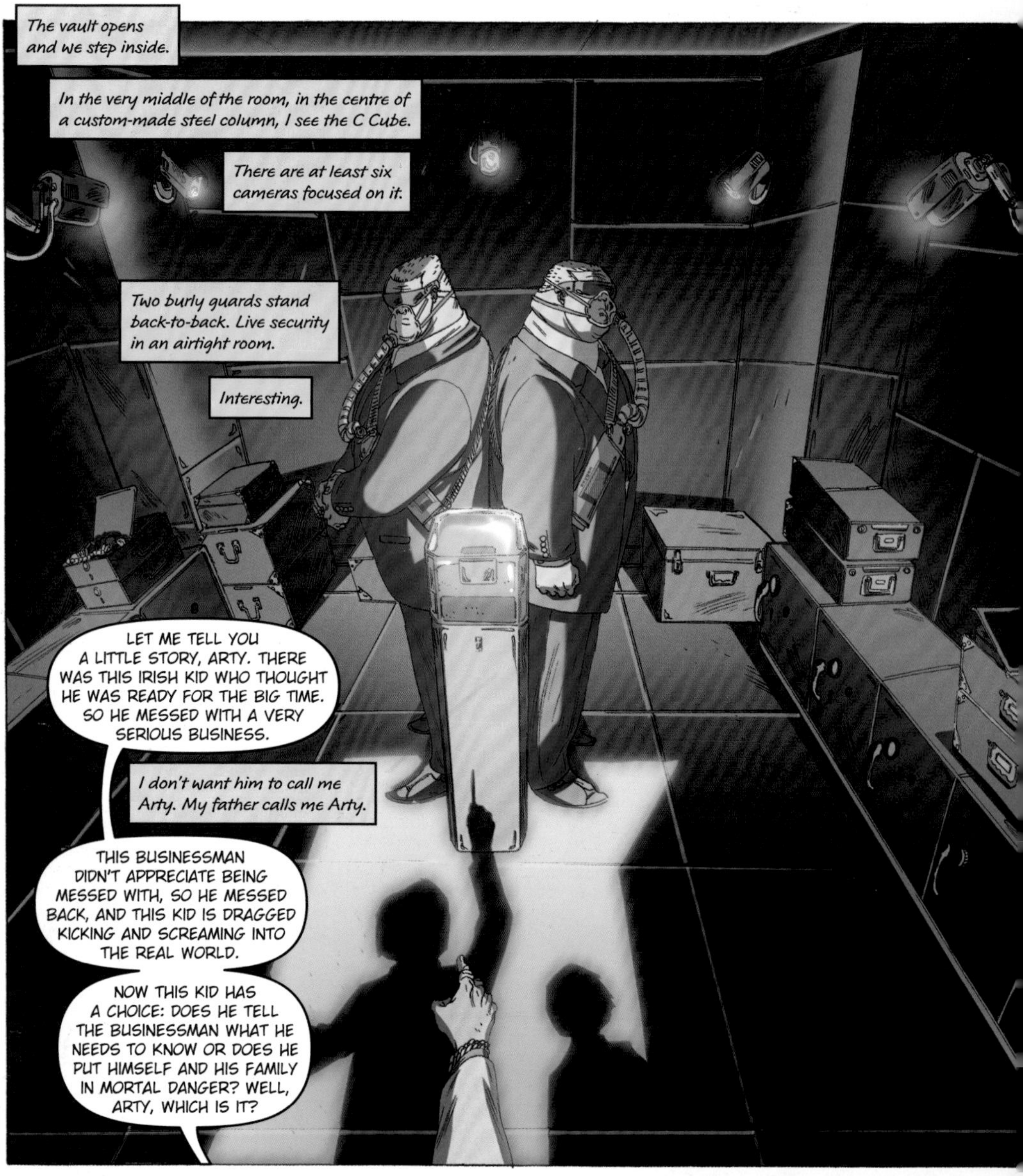
The vault opens and we step inside.
In the very middle of the room, in the centre of a custom-made steel column, I see the C Cube.
There are at least six cameras focused on it.
Two burly guards stand back-to-back. Live security in an airtight room.
Interesting.
LET ME TELL YOU A LITTLE STORY, ARTY. THERE WAS THIS IRISH KID WHO THOUGHT HE WAS READY FOR THE BIG TIME. SO HE MESSED WITH A VERY SERIOUS BUSINESS.
I don't want him to call me Arty. My father calls me Arty.
THIS BUSINESSMAN DIDN'T APPRECIATE BEING MESSED WITH, SO HE MESSED BACK, AND THIS KID IS DRAGGED KICKING AND SCREAMING INTO THE REAL WORLD.
NOW THIS KID HAS A CHOICE: DOES HE TELL THE BUSINESSMAN WHAT HE NEEDS TO KNOW OR DOES HE PUT HIMSELF AND HIS FAMILY IN MORTAL DANGER? WELL, ARTY, WHICH IS IT?

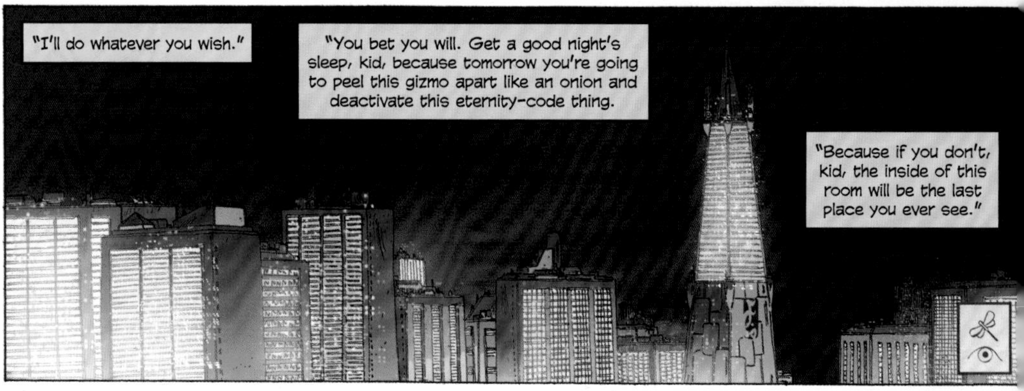
"I'll do whatever you wish."
"You bet you will. Get a good night's sleep, kid, because tomorrow you're going to peel this gizmo apart like an onion and deactivate this eternity-code thing.
"Because if you don't, kid, the inside of this room will be the last place you ever see."

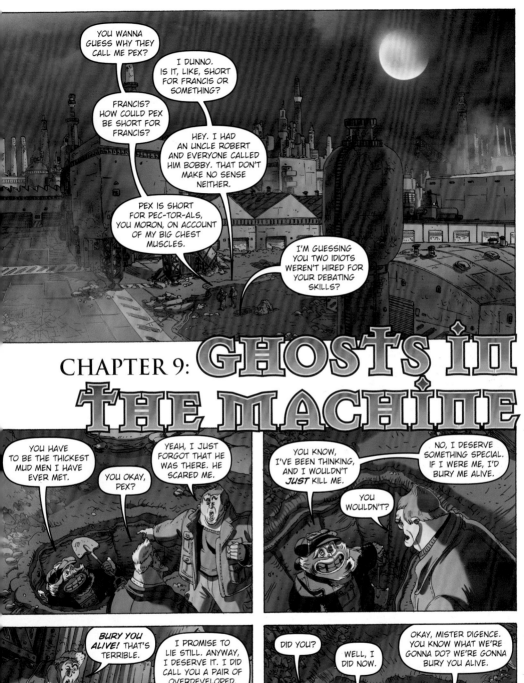

CHAPTER 9: GHOSTS IN THE MACHINE

"Idiots."

"Come on, Mulch, let's go. We have a plan, remember?"

THE SPIRO NEEDLE.

Arno Blunt walks me back to my "room".

It's comfortable enough, but it has a couple of things missing. Like windows and a handle on the door.

I DON'T KNOW WHAT HAPPENED IN THAT LONDON RESTAURANT, BUT YOU TRY THAT HERE AND I'LL TURN YOU INSIDE OUT AND EAT YOUR ORGANS.

BUTLER'S COMING FOR YOU, AND I THINK HE MIGHT HAVE SOMETHING TO SAY ABOUT THAT.

NO WAY, KID. I SAW HIM GO DOWN. I SAW THE BLOOD.

I DIDN'T SAY HE WAS ALIVE. I JUST SAID HE WAS COMING.

Blunt edges out of the room without taking his eyes off me for a second.

I'm left alone and for the first time, I feel a little anxious.

It's one thing to formulate a plan in the safety of one's own home. It is quite another to execute it while trapped in the lion's den.

My confidence has taken quite a pounding recently. Back in London, Spiro outwitted me without apparent effort.

I was so close to losing Butler that it makes me feel sick just to think about it.

Things have to change.

I remember my father's words.

"What about you, Arty? Will you make the journey with me? Will you take your chance to be a hero?"

I still don't have an answer.

The latex-covered mike hidden on my neck is still concealed and still working. I speak softly.

GOOD EVENING, FRIENDS. EVERYTHING PROCEEDS ACCORDING TO PLAN, ASSUMING THAT MULCH MADE IT BACK ALIVE.

I MUST WARN YOU TO EXPECT A VISIT FROM SPIRO'S GOONS SOON. I'M SURE HE'S MONITORING THE STREETS.

MISTER SPIRO HAS GIVEN ME A TOUR OF THE FACILITY AND HOPEFULLY YOU HAVE RECORDED EVERYTHING WE NEED TO COMPLETE OUR MISSION.

I BELIEVE THE LOCAL TERM FOR THIS KIND OF OPERATION IS HEIST.

NOW LISTEN, FRIENDS, THIS IS WHAT I WANT YOU TO DO....

SPIRO'S SECURITY CENTRE.

GOOD WORK, BOYS; YOU'LL GET THAT BONUS. NOW WE GOT A VAN THAT'S BEEN PARKED OUTSIDE FOR THREE HOURS. BEFORE THAT IT WAS SEEN CIRCLING THE BUILDING.

GET DOWN THERE. OPEN THE DOORS, SCARE EVERYTHING INSIDE, CLOSE THE DOORS. EASY.

YOU GOT IT, BOSS. AND IT'S GREAT DAT YOU GOT YA NEW TEETH OKAY.

SURE IS. WE CAN UNDERSTAND YOUZE AGAIN.

WHAT DO YA THINK?

I THINK THINGS ARE GOING OUR WAY, BUDDY. IT'S NOT EVERY DAY YOU GET A FIVE-GRAND BONUS FOR BURYING A GUY ALIVE.

UHG—DON'T REMIND ME.

HEY, MAYBE HANDLING THIS WILL BE WORTH ANOTHER FIVE-GRAND BONUS.

YEAH, FIVE AND FIVE, ALTOGETHER THAT'S... ERRR...

THAT'S A LOT OF CASH.

YEAH, A LOT OF CASH. LET'S GO SEE WHO'S IN THAT VAN.

Juliet, you awake down there?

JUST ABOUT, HOLLY. IS IT ONLY ME THAT FINDS STAKEOUTS BORING?

AGGG. HAVE YOU BEEN TALKING TO BUTLER? HE EATS UP THAT KUNG FU POP WISDOM.

Can't you "find that quiet peace at your core and inhabit it"?

WHICH, OF COURSE, MAY BE WHY BIG BROTHER HAS THE FAMOUS BLUE DIAMOND BODYGUARD TATTOO AND I DON'T.

You must learn patience, o grasshopper.

FORGET THE KUNG FU INSECTS, HOLLY, WE'RE ON. TWO HOSTILES COMING THIS WAY. BOTH BIG AND BOTH DUMB.

"You need backup?"

"Negative. I'll wrap both of them and you can have a word on your return. Let me grab my outfit."

"Okay, I'll be down in five, as soon as I've had a talk with Foaly. And, Juliet, *don't* mark them."

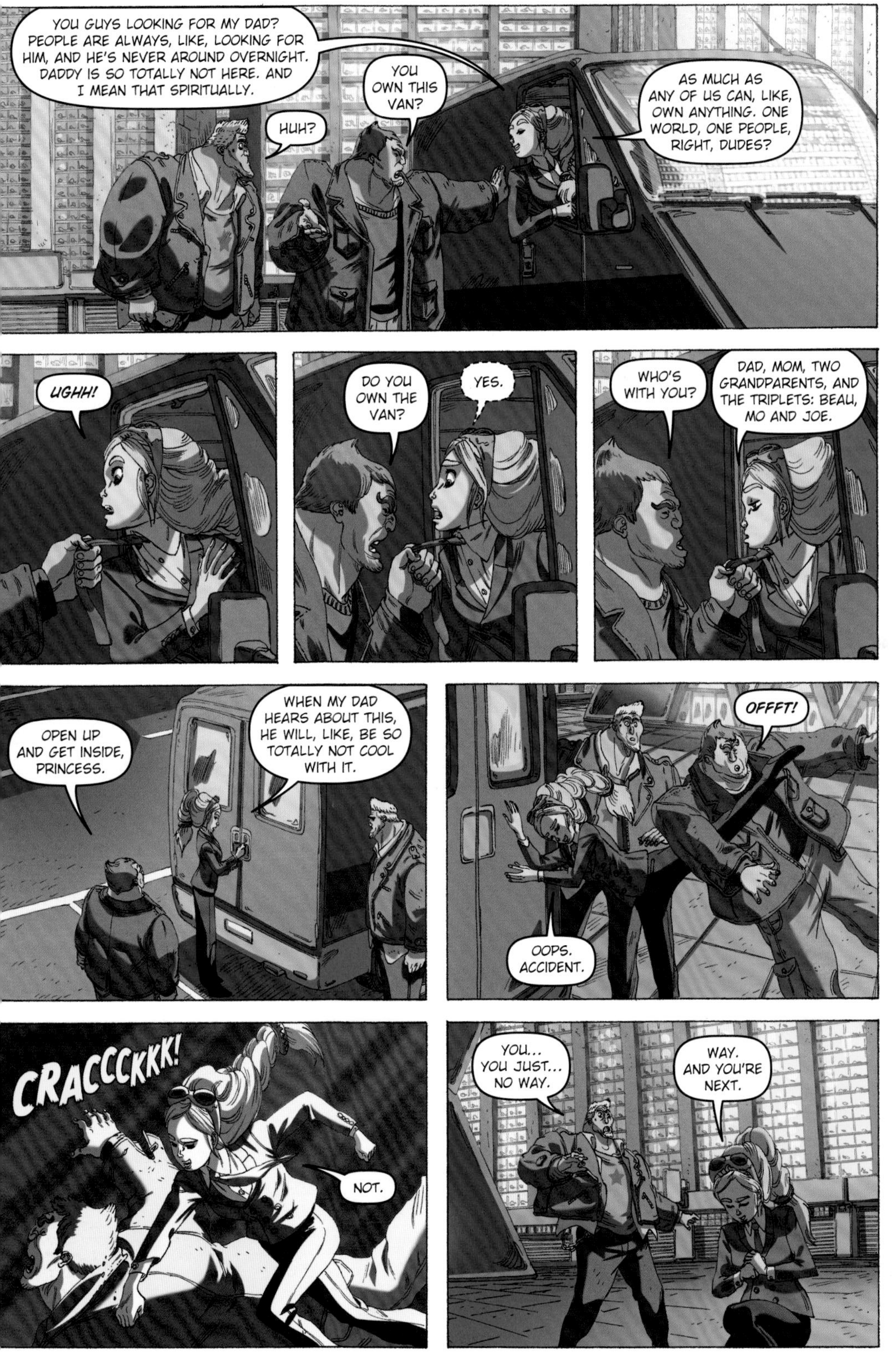
YOU GUYS LOOKING FOR MY DAD? PEOPLE ARE ALWAYS, LIKE, LOOKING FOR HIM, AND HE'S NEVER AROUND OVERNIGHT. DADDY IS SO TOTALLY NOT HERE. AND I MEAN THAT SPIRITUALLY.
HUH?
YOU OWN THIS VAN?
AS MUCH AS ANY OF US CAN, LIKE, OWN ANYTHING. ONE WORLD, ONE PEOPLE, RIGHT, DUDES?
UGHH!
DO YOU OWN THE VAN?
YES.
WHO'S WITH YOU?
DAD, MOM, TWO GRANDPARENTS, AND THE TRIPLETS: BEAU, MO AND JOE.
OPEN UP AND GET INSIDE, PRINCESS.
WHEN MY DAD HEARS ABOUT THIS, HE WILL, LIKE, BE SO TOTALLY NOT COOL WITH IT.
OFFFT!
OOPS. ACCIDENT.
CRACCCKKK!
NOT.
YOU... YOU JUST... NO WAY.
WAY. AND YOU'RE NEXT.

Juliet is a piece of work. A chip off the Butler block.

But she's also a wild card. Even on stakeout she can't stop chattering for more than ten seconds. None of her brother's discipline.

She's a kid who shouldn't be in this line of work. And Artemis has no business dragging her into his crazy schemes.

But then, I can't talk. I'm about to break the rules for the hundredth time to help him. There was something about the Irish boy that makes you forget your reservations.

FOALY. YOU THERE?

I heard you. Perfect timing. I've just been watching the end of the goblin general's trial. Guilty on all counts, thanks to you. Sentencing is next month.

GUILTY. THANK THE SPIRITS.

Opal is still doing her coma act, so Haven City waits with bated breath to see what happens with that psychopath. Anyway, why the call, Holly? Feeling homesick?

NO, NOT HOMESICK.

I JUST NEED YOUR ADVICE.

Advice? Oh, really? That wouldn't be a sneaky way of asking for help, now, would it? You heard what Commander Root said.

YES, FOALY. RULES ARE RULES. I KNOW. I SAID TO ARTEMIS YOU PROBABLY WOULDN'T WANT TO HELP. THE SPIRO NEEDLE IS A FORTRESS. THERE'S NO WAY IN WITHOUT YOU..

No way in, eh?

EVEN ARTEMIS ADMITS IT. "WE CAN'T DO IT WITHOUT FOALY," HIS EXACT WORDS. WE'RE NOT LOOKING FOR EQUIPMENT OR EXTRA FAIRY-POWER. JUST ADVICE OVER THE AIRWAVES, MAYBE A BIT OF CAMERA WORK.

Hmmm...You got any video?

IT WILL BE IN YOUR MAINFRAME IN TWO MINUTES, ALONG WITH A 3-D X-RAY SCAN OF THE WHOLE BUILDING.

Fowl is right. Without me you're sunk.

I'll help. But no guarantees.

You're going to miss him when this is over and Fowl's mind is wiped, aren't you?

I say "No", but my eyes tell a different story.

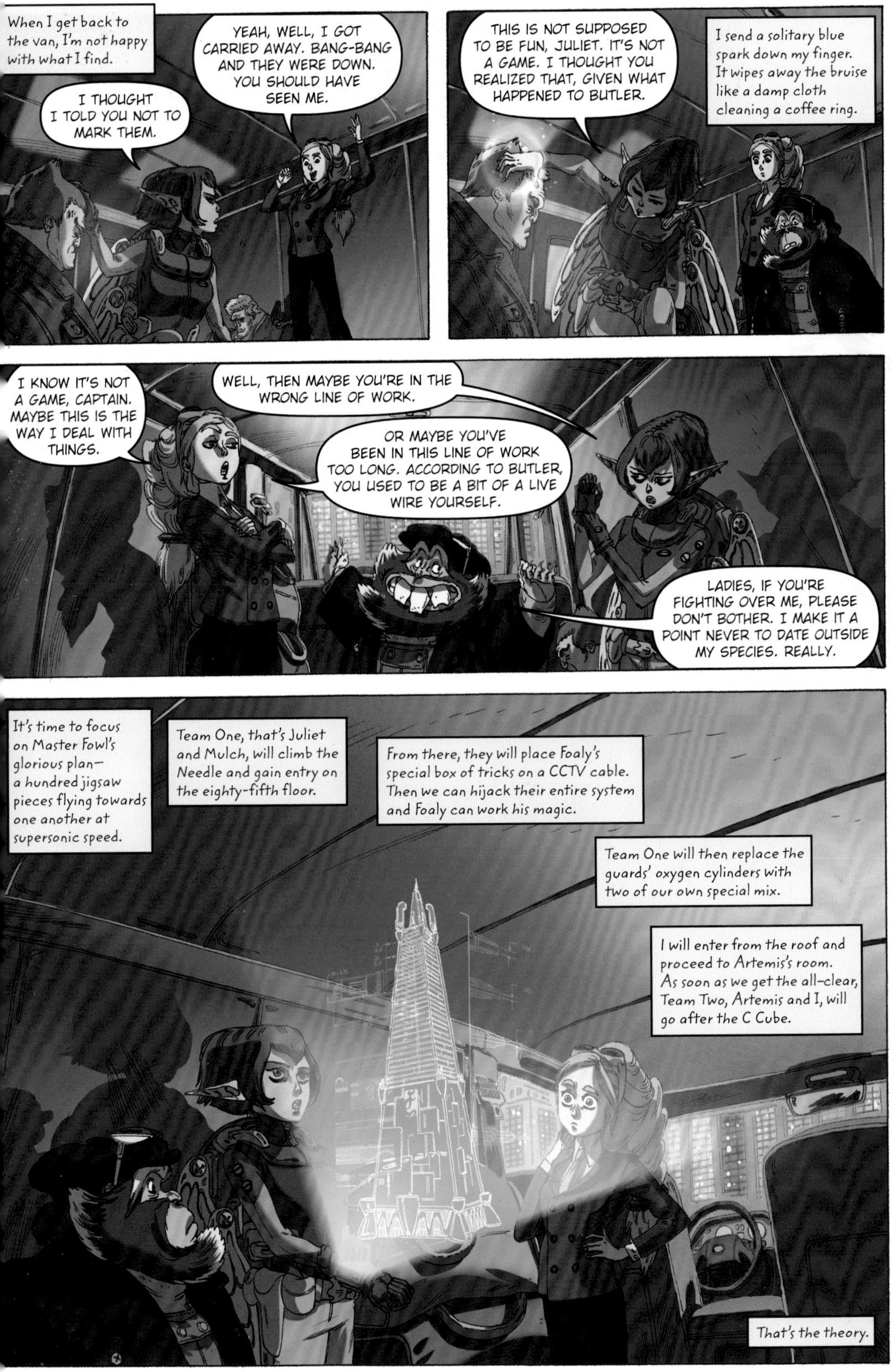
When I get back to the van, I'm not happy with what I find.
I THOUGHT I TOLD YOU NOT TO MARK THEM.
YEAH, WELL, I GOT CARRIED AWAY. BANG-BANG AND THEY WERE DOWN. YOU SHOULD HAVE SEEN ME.
THIS IS NOT SUPPOSED TO BE FUN, JULIET. IT'S NOT A GAME. I THOUGHT YOU REALIZED THAT, GIVEN WHAT HAPPENED TO BUTLER.
I send a solitary blue spark down my finger. It wipes away the bruise like a damp cloth cleaning a coffee ring.
I KNOW IT'S NOT A GAME, CAPTAIN. MAYBE THIS IS THE WAY I DEAL WITH THINGS.
WELL, THEN MAYBE YOU'RE IN THE WRONG LINE OF WORK.
OR MAYBE YOU'VE BEEN IN THIS LINE OF WORK TOO LONG. ACCORDING TO BUTLER, YOU USED TO BE A BIT OF A LIVE WIRE YOURSELF.
LADIES, IF YOU'RE FIGHTING OVER ME, PLEASE DON'T BOTHER. I MAKE IT A POINT NEVER TO DATE OUTSIDE MY SPECIES. REALLY.
It's time to focus on Master Fowl's glorious plan—a hundred jigsaw pieces flying towards one another at supersonic speed.
Team One, that's Juliet and Mulch, will climb the Needle and gain entry on the eighty-fifth floor.
From there, they will place Foaly's special box of tricks on a CCTV cable. Then we can hijack their entire system and Foaly can work his magic.
Team One will then replace the guards' oxygen cylinders with two of our own special mix.
I will enter from the roof and proceed to Artemis's room. As soon as we get the all-clear, Team Two, Artemis and I, will go after the C Cube.
That's the theory.

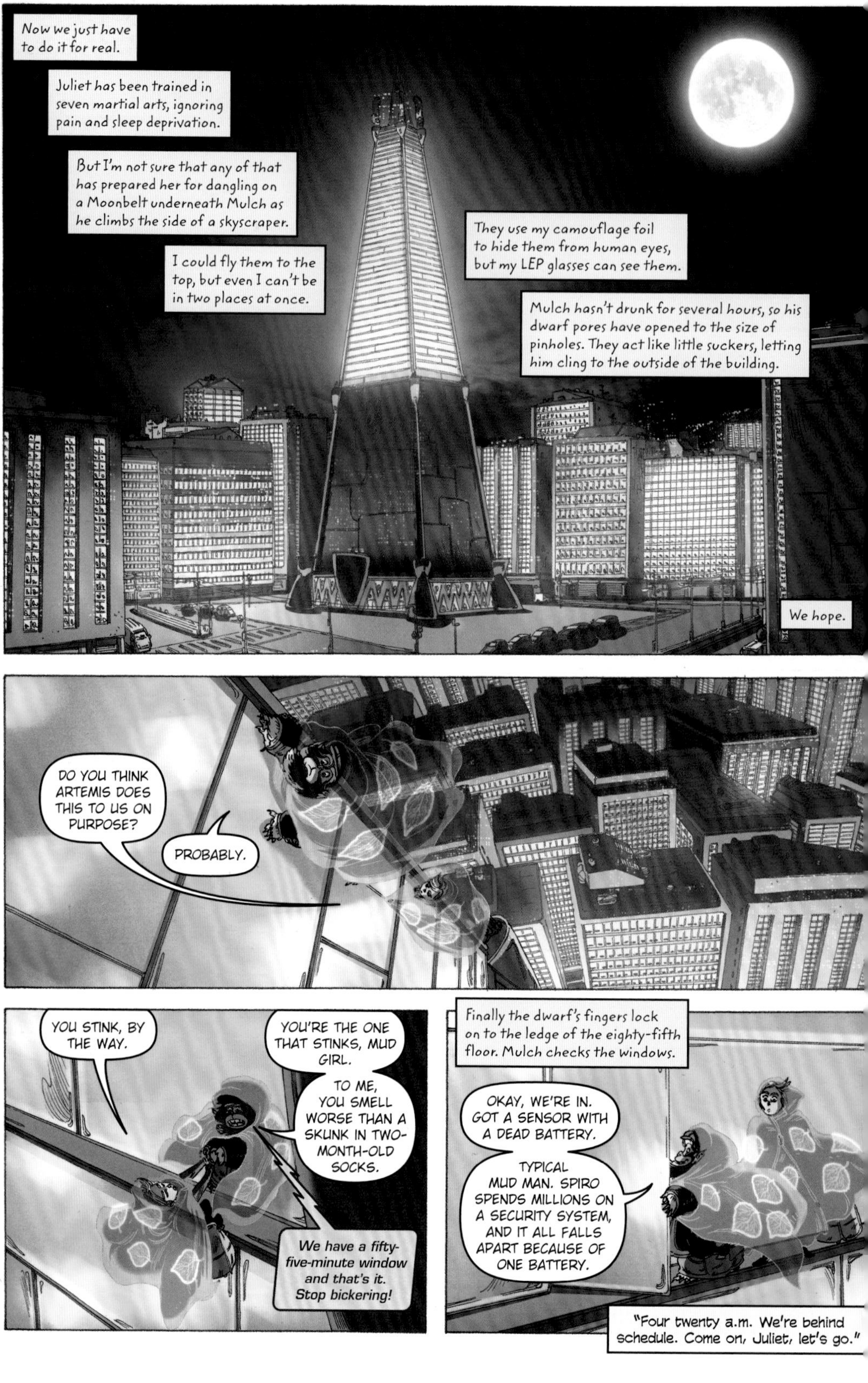

Now we just have to do it for real.
Juliet has been trained in seven martial arts, ignoring pain and sleep deprivation.
But I'm not sure that any of that has prepared her for dangling on a Moonbelt underneath Mulch as he climbs the side of a skyscraper.
I could fly them to the top, but even I can't be in two places at once.
They use my camouflage foil to hide them from human eyes, but my LEP glasses can see them.
Mulch hasn't drunk for several hours, so his dwarf pores have opened to the size of pinholes. They act like little suckers, letting him cling to the outside of the building.
We hope.
DO YOU THINK ARTEMIS DOES THIS TO US ON PURPOSE?
PROBABLY.
YOU STINK, BY THE WAY.
YOU'RE THE ONE THAT STINKS, MUD GIRL.
TO ME, YOU SMELL WORSE THAN A SKUNK IN TWO-MONTH-OLD SOCKS.
We have a fifty-five-minute window and that's it. Stop bickering!
Finally the dwarf's fingers lock on to the ledge of the eighty-fifth floor. Mulch checks the windows.
OKAY, WE'RE IN. GOT A SENSOR WITH A DEAD BATTERY.
TYPICAL MUD MAN. SPIRO SPENDS MILLIONS ON A SECURITY SYSTEM, AND IT ALL FALLS APART BECAUSE OF ONE BATTERY.
"Four twenty a.m. We're behind schedule. Come on, Juliet, let's go."

I'm preparing for my own part in the plan as well as following Mulch and Juliet's progress at the same time. Distracting isn't the word.

WAIT! THE CAMERA!

Juliet nearly walks straight into view of one of Spiro's CCTV cameras. Concentrate, girl, concentrate.

They need to get to the camera's video cable to put Foaly's magic box in place.

THE CAMO FOIL DOESN'T WORK ON CAMERAS—ONLY ON HUMAN EYES.

OH, THAT'S USEFUL.

Six metres of corridor between success and failure.

YOU'RE NOT SERIOUS.

DEADLY. WE NEED TO NUDGE THE CAMERA OVER A BIT WITHOUT DAMAGING IT. YOU GOT A BETTER IDEA?

PUUUT!

Mulch's wind offensive blows the camera out of line. The corridor is clear and Juliet puts Foaly's video clip where it needs to go.

SO, FOALY, DO I JUST JAM IT AROUND THE CABLES?

Careful! That is a very, very complex piece of nanotechnology. Basically yes, just jam it in.

PERFECT! WE HAVE EYES AND EARS.

OKAY, AND THIS REALLY IS ME BEING A GENIUS, I'M ABOUT TO COMPLETELY WIPE MOVING PATTERNS FROM ALL THE SURVEILLANCE FOOTAGE. YOU KEEP MOVING AND YOU'RE INVISIBLE.

OKAY, NOW WE REPLACE THE OXYGEN CYLINDERS. THE SECURITY CENTRE IS ONE CORRIDOR OVER. WE TAKE THE SHORTEST ROUTE.

PLAN SAYS DOWN THIS CORRIDOR AND TWO RIGHT TURNS.

I SAID THE SHORTEST ROUTE. THINK LATERALLY.

KA-CRUNNNNCH!

Mulch bites his way through the office of the Vice President of International Loans and Refinancing Options. I have to admit, for a non-LEP operative, the dwarf is quite effective.

Now all they have to do is swap two oxygen canisters. Of course, our new ones don't contain oxygen.

OKAY, THIS IS WHERE I EARN MY KEEP. YOU STAY HERE.

There's only one guard on duty and he's being entertained by a rerun of last night's basketball game. Good.

Juliet stops for breath and her fuzzy outline appears on a monitor for a second.

Keep moving, Juliet, or you'll be spotted!

Juliet reaches up slowly and slips the two substitute canisters into the rack.

EASY DOES IT.

"Okay, Mulch. Mission accomplished. Tell Holly."

I'm shielded and hovering six metres above the Spiro Needle, waiting for the green light.

Go. I say again, we have a go situation on the black-op code-red thing.

Mulch goes into a giggling fit and I turn off his com link.

There are far too many variables for me to ever be comfortable with this operation.

I really wouldn't be here at all if it weren't vital to the future of fairy civilization.

Artemis saw Spiro do this earlier. I watched a slow-motion replay and got the entry code. With Spiro's invitation earlier, I'm in.

THANK YOU, SPIRO.

I KNOW YOU DON'T HAVE ENOUGH ON YOUR MIND, HOLLY, BUT IF YOU WANT THE LATEST NEWS...

IT SEEMS THAT OPAL KOBOI IS GOING TO BE KEPT IN THE J. ARGON CLINIC UNTIL SHE WAKES. OR STOPS FAKING A COMA—WHICHEVER IS SOONER.

"Great."

I put that psychotic pixie out of my mind and step inside. There are cameras every six metres, but they can't see through my fairy shield, unlike the camo foil.

"Keep going, Holly. Artemis is on floor eighty-four. The vault is on eighty-five; Spiro's penthouse is on eighty-six, where you are now."

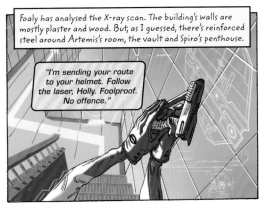

Foaly has analysed the X-ray scan. The building's walls are mostly plaster and wood. But, as I guessed, there's reinforced steel around Artemis's room, the vault and Spiro's penthouse.

"I'm sending your route to your helmet. Follow the laser, Holly. Foolproof. No offence."

The red laser leads me down a floor and to a locked office.

I'VE HAD TO UNSHIELD TO PICK THIS LOCK. ARE YOU SURE MY PATTERN IS WIPED FROM THE VIDEO?

A. Ronam

Felcor
alanna
Nogari

Of course it is.

I can imagine the childish pout on Foaly's lips.

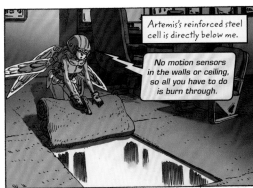

Artemis's reinforced steel cell is directly below me.

No motion sensors in the walls or ceiling, so all you have to do is burn through.

I set the room's air conditioning to "extract" to stop the fire alarm from going off.

Then I adjust my Neutrino's output, concentrating the beam so that it cuts through the metal floor.

Smoke billows from the molten gash.

Sweat streams down my face.

I'M CUTTING THE FINAL SECTION NOW.

"Won't that make a lot of noise when it falls?"

"I doubt it."

ARTEMIS FOWL'S CELL, THE SPIRO NEEDLE.

I am meditating when the first laser stroke cuts through the ceiling.

I have already arranged some pillows on the floor. Holly has guessed I'd silence the impact.

CHAPTER 10: FINGERS AND THUMBS

YOU ANTICIPATED MY PLAN.

ONLY THIRTEEN AND ALREADY PREDICTABLE.

EXACTLY. I THINK WE'RE GETTING TO KNOW EACH OTHER RATHER TOO WELL.

I PRESUME YOU USED THE AIR CONDITIONER TO VACUUM AWAY THE SMOKE?

Holly pulls me up, then gives me an earpiece.

DO WE HAVE MISTER FOALY ON OUR SIDE?

ASK HIM YOURSELF.

Well, Foaly. Astound me.

YOU'RE GOING TO LOVE THIS, MUD BOY. NOT ONLY HAVE I WIPED YOUR ESCAPE FROM THE CCTV SYSTEM, BUT I'VE CREATED A SIM OF YOU WHO'S STILL ASLEEP IN BED.

OKAY. LET'S GET GOING. WE NEED TO REACH SPIRO IN HIS APARTMENT BEFORE THE GUARDS CHANGE SO WE CAN SCAN HIS RETINA AND THUMB.

THE SCANS... YES.

An expression flashes across the human boy's face. Guilt?

IS THERE SOMETHING YOU'RE NOT TELLING ME?

NO, CAPTAIN SHORT. NOTHING.

ARTEMIS. IF YOU MESS WITH ME NOW, IN THE MIDDLE OF AN OPERATION, I WON'T FORGET IT.

DON'T WORRY, *I* WILL. COME ON.

Holly burns through to the floor above where Spiro's apartment is.

We climb up and find ourselves in a small, dark space full of white shirts.

We're inside his closet.

Okay, there are no cameras inside Spiro's own apartment. You're clear.

Better put Spiro to sleep.

HE *IS* ASLEEP. IT'S TEN TO FIVE IN THE MORNING.

Well, better make sure he doesn't wake up, then.

Holly uses a *Sleeper Deeper* capsule to hijack Spiro's brain waves and keep him snoring. More priceless fairy tech.

The room is so white it nearly glows in the dark. Futuristic furniture—white of course. White spotlights. White drapes.

The picture is in oils. Completely white. It's called "Snow Ghost".

OH, GIVE ME A BREAK.

snow ghost

Spiro is dead to the world, just as Holly promised. Even in his sleep, he looks malevolent.

Holly's helmet camera scans Spiro's eye.

Now for the tough part.

OKAY, EYE SCAN DONE. NOW WE TAKE AN IMPRINT OF HIS THUMBPRINT USING A LATEX BANDAGE—JUST LIKE YOU SUGGESTED, GENIUS BOY.

IT WON'T WORK.

WHAT?

THE IMPRINT WILL BE IN REVERSE. LIKE A PHOTO NEGATIVE. RIDGES WHERE THERE SHOULD BE GROOVES. I'M AMAZED NO ONE ELSE SPOTTED THE FLAW IN THE PLAN.

WHAT? YOU KNEW THIS ALL ALONG? SO WHY LIE?

THERE'S NO WAY TO FOOL THE GEL SCANNER. IT HAS TO BE THE REAL THUMB.

D'ARVIT! WHAT DO YOU WANT ME TO DO? CUT OFF HIS THUMB AND TAKE IT WITH US??

Artemis's silence says it all.

LISTEN TO ME, CAPTAIN. IT'S ONLY A TEMPORARY MEASURE. THE THUMB CAN BE REATTACHED. TRUE?

JUST SHUT UP, ARTEMIS. AND I THOUGHT YOU'D CHANGED.

FOUR MINUTES. WE HAVE FOUR MINUTES TO CRACK THE VAULT AND GET BACK. CLASSIC HEALING TIME.

SPIRO WON'T FEEL A THING.

FOALY, ARE YOU LISTENING TO THIS INSANITY?

It sounds insane, Holly. But if we don't get the technology in the C Cube back, we could lose a whole lot more than a thumb.

Agggg.

Artemis is manipulating the People to his own ends. Again.

Fifteen-centimetre beam.

ONE CUT. CLEAN.

SHUT UP, BOTH OF YOU.

I see Artemis check behind Spiro's ears.

HMM. CLEVER.

WHAT NOW?

NOTHING IMPORTANT. PLEASE CONTINUE.

I send a gentle pulse of magic into the hand.

The Sleeper Deeper pill is more efficient than any anaesthetic.

But this isn't what magic should be used for.

I make the cut.

Not one drop of blood is spilled.

"Nice work, Captain Short. Let's go. The clock is ticking."

We head to the vault. Holly doesn't speak to me unless she has to.

Almost a mile and a half of corridor of this floor and six guards patrolling it at any one time.

ARE YOU CERTAIN THEY'RE MESMERIZED? THEY DON'T LOOK MESMERIZED.

THAT'S BECAUSE I'M VERY, VERY GOOD.

CAPTAIN HOOK WOULD KICK BARNEY'S PURPLE BUTT TEN TIMES OUT OF TEN.

YOU'RE MISSING THE WHOLE POINT OF BARNEY. IT'S A VALUES THING. BUTT-KICKING IS NOT THE ISSUE.

IT'S OKAY. THEY'RE MESMERIZED NOT TO NOTICE ANYBODY OUT OF THE ORDINARY ON THIS FLOOR.

NOT UNLESS THEY'RE DIRECTLY POINTED OUT TO THEM.

You have sixty seconds until the next set of unmesmerized guards turns the corner. They will see you both instantly.

OKAY, FOALY, HERE WE GO.

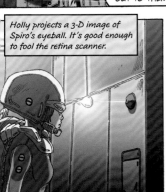

Holly projects a 3-D image of Spiro's eyeball. It's good enough to fool the retina scanner.

Next is Foaly's pitch-perfect recording....

Jon Spiro. I am the boss, so open up quick.

Lastly, Holly gives me a cold look and presses the severed thumb against the scanner.

It's the longest half second of my life until there's a very satisfying...

CLICK!

We're in.

GO AND REATTACH THE THUMB. I'M RIGHT BEHIND YOU.

AND IF YOU'RE NOT?

WE GO TO PLAN B.

LET'S HOPE WE DON'T HAVE TO.

Holly disappears down the corridor and the vault door slides shut behind me.

Both happen before the next set of guards appear.

The plan is working.

There's now enough air in the vault to last the few minutes that I need.

I ignore the jewels and the bearer bonds, and go straight for the Cube.

I HOPE YOU GENTLEMEN DON'T MIND IF I BORROW MISTER SPIRO'S CUBE FOR A WHILE?

The men stay unnaturally still. All thanks to the paralytic gas in the oxygen tanks delivered by Juliet.

As I reach for the C Cube, something moves in the background.

There's a pneumatic hiss....

SPIRO'S BEDROOM.

The healing only takes a few seconds. Threads of blue light stitch the flesh and bone together.

A few stray sparks skip along Spiro's body up towards the areas behind both ears.

FOALY, THERE ARE MATCHING SCARS BEHIND SPIRO'S EARS....

Surgery. Maybe Spiro got himself a facelift.

YEAH, EITHER THAT OR— *THIS ISN'T SPIRO!*

A false wall slides away to reveal the real Jon Spiro, and at his side, Blunt.

BRAVO, MASTER FOWL. SOME OF US DIDN'T THINK YOU'D MAKE IT THIS FAR. THAT'S A HUNDRED BUCKS YOU OWE ME, ARNO.

THE SPIRO UPSTAIRS IS MY COUSIN. ONE OR TWO COSMETIC CUTS AND WE'RE PEAS IN A POD. JUST FOR TONIGHT, I SET THE GEL SCANNER TO ACCEPT HIS PRINT. I WANTED TO SEE HOW FAR YOU WERE GOING TO GET.

YOU'RE AN AMAZING KID, ARTY. NO ONE EVER MADE IT INTO THE VAULT BEFORE.

HOW DID YOU DO IT?

TRADE SECRET.

YEAH? WELL, WE'LL REVIEW THE CAMERA FOOTAGE.

CHECK HIM FOR AN EARPIECE, ARNO.

It takes Blunt less than five seconds to find the earpiece. He crushes it under his boot. I take the chance to spook him. Again.

BUTLER IS STILL COMING FOR YOU.

BUTLER IS DEAD. I SAW HIM GO DOWN.

THE KID IS MESSING WITH YOUR MIND, ARNO. GET YOURSELF A SPINE.

ALL THIS TOUGH TALK AND REPARTEE HAS BEEN FUN, ARTY. BUT I DON'T HAVE TIME FOR ANY MORE GAMES.

NOW LISTEN CAREFULLY, KID. I WANT YOU TO UNLOCK THE CUBE. NO MORE BLARNEY.

YOU GET THIS BABY WORKING FOR ME RIGHT NOW.

CLICK

I open up the Cube. Spiro's eyes are wide with anticipation and dreams of wealth.

What I'm really doing is taking out the fairy tech blocker and giving Foaly remote access to the Cube.

I am not a box. I am a marvel of artificial intelligence. I live, therefore I learn!

IS THE BOX WORKING YET?

I HAD TO REVERT TO VERSION 1.0. LESS SECURE AND A BIT MORE TEMPERAMENTAL.

Spiro starts by asking the Cube questions he already has the answers to.

Foaly instantly sources the info and suddenly it looks like the all-knowing Cube is obeying Spiro's every whim.

WHAT ABOUT THAT GROUP, THE LEP, CUBE? THEY WERE MONITORING ME IN LONDON. ARE THEY STILL WATCHING?

The LEP? That's a Lebanese satellite TV network. Game shows mostly. Their footprint doesn't reach this far.

Foaly follows the script perfectly. That's ended Spiro's curiosity about the LEP.

Spiro opens the vault door and Pex and Chips appear.

MISTER SPIRO. IS THIS SOME KIND OF DRILL?

OH, LOOK, HERE COMES THE CAVALRY.

I'D LOVE TO KNOW HOW LITTLE ARTEMIS HERE GOT PAST YOU TWO.

The hired muscle stare at me as if I have just appeared from nowhere. Which, for their poor mesmerized brains, I have.

WHERE DID HE COME FROM? HE WASN'T... BUT...

YOU KNOW WHAT? I RECKON I'VE GOT TWENTY YEARS LEFT IN ME. AFTER THAT THE WORLD CAN GO TO HELL AS FAR AS I'M CONCERNED.

I DON'T HAVE ANY FAMILY, NO HEIRS. NO NEED TO BUILD FOR THE FUTURE. SO I'M GONNA USE THIS CUBE TO SUCK THIS PLANET DRY.

I KNOW THE FIRST THING I'D DO.

BUY YOURSELF A BOOTH AT MERV'S RIB 'N' ROAST?

NO, I'D STICK IT TO THOSE PHONETIX GUYS.

THEY'VE BEEN RUBBING SPIRO INDUSTRIES' NOSE IN IT FOR YEARS.

PHONETIX. MY BIGGEST COMPETITORS. YOU KNOW, NOTHING WOULD GIVE ME GREATER SATISFACTION THAN TO DESTROY THAT BUNCH OF SECOND-RATE PHONE FREAKS. BUT HOW?

Hey, boss man. I'm the most powerful Cube in the world, remember?

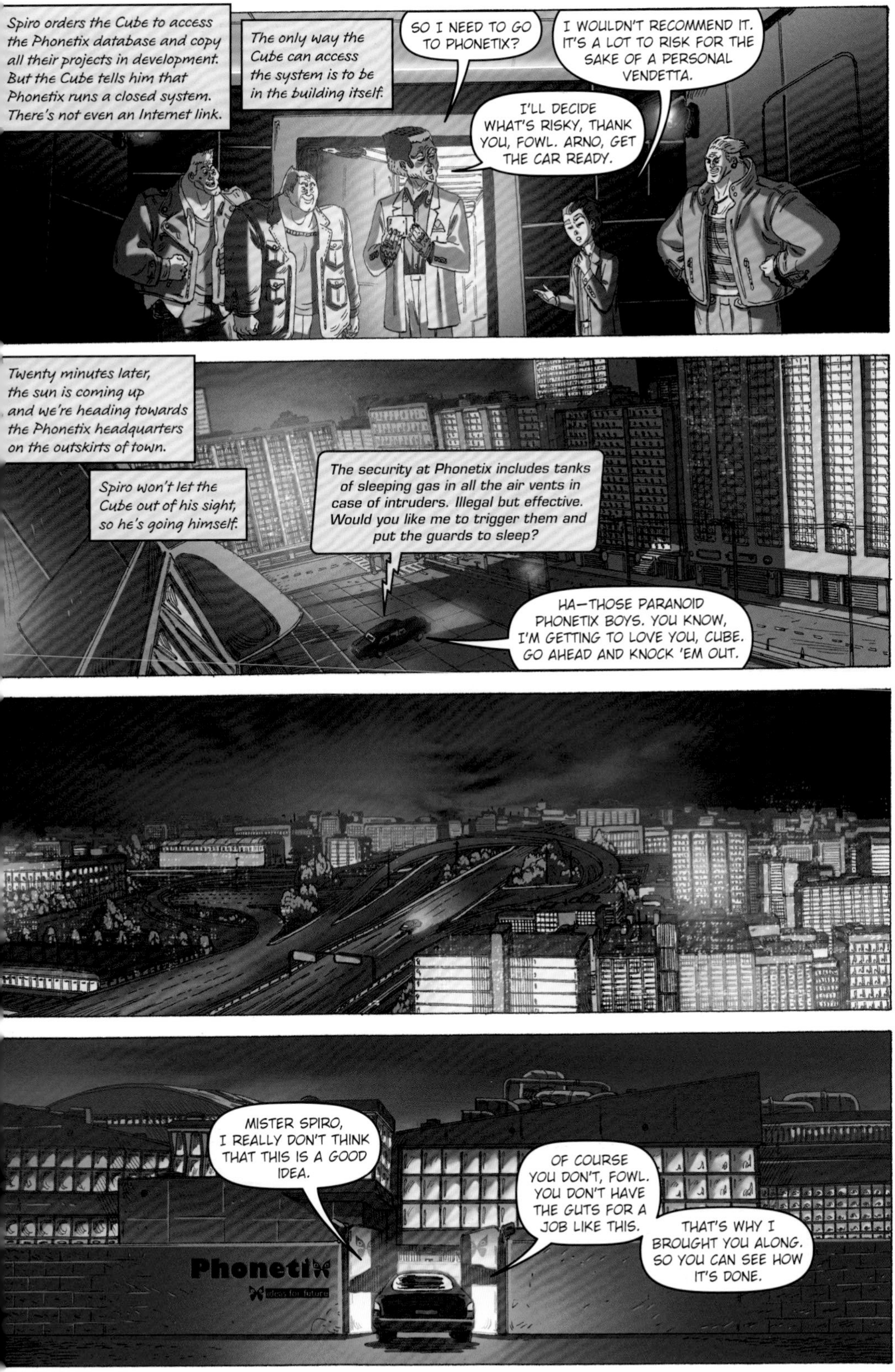
Spiro orders the Cube to access the Phonetix database and copy all their projects in development. But the Cube tells him that Phonetix runs a closed system. There's not even an Internet link.
The only way the Cube can access the system is to be in the building itself.
SO I NEED TO GO TO PHONETIX?
I WOULDN'T RECOMMEND IT. IT'S A LOT TO RISK FOR THE SAKE OF A PERSONAL VENDETTA.
I'LL DECIDE WHAT'S RISKY, THANK YOU, FOWL. ARNO, GET THE CAR READY.
Twenty minutes later, the sun is coming up and we're heading towards the Phonetix headquarters on the outskirts of town.
Spiro won't let the Cube out of his sight, so he's going himself.
The security at Phonetix includes tanks of sleeping gas in all the air vents in case of intruders. Illegal but effective. Would you like me to trigger them and put the guards to sleep?
HA—THOSE PARANOID PHONETIX BOYS. YOU KNOW, I'M GETTING TO LOVE YOU, CUBE. GO AHEAD AND KNOCK 'EM OUT.
MISTER SPIRO, I REALLY DON'T THINK THAT THIS IS A GOOD IDEA.
OF COURSE YOU DON'T, FOWL. YOU DON'T HAVE THE GUTS FOR A JOB LIKE THIS.
THAT'S WHY I BROUGHT YOU ALONG. SO YOU CAN SEE HOW IT'S DONE.
Phonetix
ideas for future

The Cube remote-activates the door entry and lets our band of intruders into the lobby.

No alarms sound. No platoon of security guards rushes to detain us.

The research lab is eight floors below us, underground. Elevator entry ahead.

Phonetix

FINALLY, I'M GONNA PUT PHONETIX OUT OF BUSINESS.

I GOTTA ADMIT IT, MISTER SPIRO. THIS IS BEAUTIFUL.

PHONETIX EVEN FOOTS THE BILL FOR THE SLEEPING GAS.

HOLLY, THIS IS JULIET. SPIRO IS IN THE ELEVATOR. ARTEMIS IS WITH HIM. THREE GOONS.

Understood. Time to make that call.

WE'RE GOING UNDERGROUND WHERE THE DINOSAUR BONES ARE. DID YOU KNOW THAT AFTER A MILLION BILLION YEARS DINOSAUR DUNG TURNS INTO DIAMONDS?

NO, I DIDN'T KNOW THAT, PEX. MAYBE I SHOULD PAY YOUR WAGES IN DUNG. YOU LIKE THAT IDEA?

The lab itself is protected by a simple key code. It takes the Cube seconds to crack it.

EASY. I SHOULD HAVE DONE THIS YEARS AGO.

LOOKS LIKE ALL THE GUARDS ARE UNCONSCIOUS, MISTER SPIRO.

SPEAKING OF CAMERAS, WE'RE GOING TO HAVE TO RAID THE VIDEO ROOM ON THE WAY OUT. GET RID OF ANY TAPES THAT SHOW US.

No need. I have already wiped all your images from the security recordings.

I'M LIKING YOU MORE AND MORE, CUBE. SO, WHAT HAPPENS NOW?

Foaly tells Spiro to put the Cube on the monolithic hard drive and stalls for time until...

Download complete. We have every Phonetix project for the next decade.

YOU TRAITOR, CUBE!

BEAUTIFUL. I'M SO HAPPY YOU'RE HERE TO SEE THIS MOMENT, FOWL, BECAUSE RIGHT NOW I'M...HEY.

WHAT'S WRONG WITH YOUR EYES? THEY DON'T MATCH.

Spiro plucks the iris-cam from my eye.

WHAT IS THIS?

EH, MISTER SPIRO...

I DON'T KNOW WHAT THIS DOES, FOWL. BUT YOU WON'T BE LEAVING HERE ALIVE.

MISTER SPIRO, PLEASE...

WHAT IS IT, BLUNT? WHAT DO YOU WANT?

"I think we have a situation outside, sir."

Phonetix

01 02 03 04 05

Juliet did it.

UNIT THREE IN POSITION. WE'RE GOING IN.

There was no sleeping gas. There are no sleeping guards. Only Juliet acting the part. Holly got her here in time for our Plan B.

Looks like the Chicago P.D. has brought everything they have.

Good.

Phonetix is one of the top five subscribers to the Police Benevolent Fund—I'd expect nothing less.

I check that Juliet's ready.

Juliet? Heads up. Cops about to enter the building.

I SEE THEM, HOLLY.

Of course, she is.

SECURITY JACKET DUMPED, POLICE JACKET DEPLOYED.

I'LL WAIT UNTIL THE COPS ARE INSIDE, THEN JOIN THEIR GROUP.

Good. Keep your head down and wait for my signal.

I'm delighted to see the officers of the law make an appearance.

Spiro and Blunt, less so.

SWAT. HELICOPTERS. HEAVY ARMAMENT. HOW DID THIS HAPPEN?

YOU SET ME UP, FOWL. THIS ENTIRE THING.

BUT HOW? IT'S NOT POSSIBLE.

OBVIOUSLY IT IS. I KNEW YOU WOULD BE WAITING FOR ME IN THE SPIRO NEEDLE VAULT. AFTER THAT, ALL I HAD TO DO WAS USE YOUR OWN HATRED OF PHONETIX TO LURE YOU HERE, OUT OF YOUR CAREFULLY CONTROLLED ENVIRONMENT.

I DON'T GET IT, FOWL. IF I GO DOWN FOR BREAKING IN HERE, THEN SO DO YOU.

NO. I'M NOT EVEN HERE. TAKE A LOOK AT THE TAPES.

Thanks to Foaly's magic, the replays show Spiro entering the building, but I'm nowhere to be seen.

IT'S TRUE, MISTER SPIRO. HE AIN'T THERE NO MORE.

WHAT?!

EXCUSE ME, SIR. LET ME SLIDE DOWN ON THE CABLES. I'LL BLOW OPEN THE ELEVATOR DOORS AND THEN YOU CUT THE POWER.

NO— MUCH, MUCH TOO DANGEROUS. WHO ARE YOU, ANYWAY?

SORRY, SIR. I'M NEW. AND RATHER IMPULSIVE.

HEY!

From above, I see Spiro start to lose it.

His whole body vibrates and spittle sprays from his lips in a wide arc.

I SUPPOSE MO DIGENCE WAS WORKING FOR YOU, TOO?

YES. PEX AND CHIPS TOO, EVEN IF THEY DIDN'T KNOW IT. YOU WOULD NEVER HAVE COME HERE IF I HAD SUGGESTED IT.

I watch, blaster in hand.

Plan B is making me more nervous than Plan A ever did.

The Mud Boy's whole scheme has been fraught with risk.

If Spiro had decided to shoot Artemis inside the Spiro Needle, then it was all over.

But no, just as Artemis had predicted, Spiro had opted to gloat for as long as possible. Typical human.

The Mud Boy has orchestrated this whole operation from beginning to end.

It had even been his idea to mesmerize Pex and Chips. It was crucial that they plant the idea to invade Phonetix.

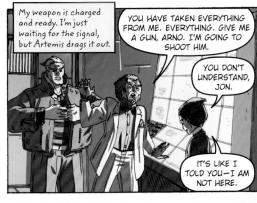

My weapon is charged and ready. I'm just waiting for the signal, but Artemis drags it out.

YOU HAVE TAKEN EVERYTHING FROM ME. EVERYTHING. GIVE ME A GUN, ARNO. I'M GOING TO SHOOT HIM.

YOU DON'T UNDERSTAND, JON.

IT'S LIKE I TOLD YOU—I AM NOT HERE.

AND ABOUT MY NAME...ARTEMIS IS GENERALLY A FEMALE NAME, AFTER THE GREEK GODDESS OF ARCHERY. BUT EVERY NOW AND THEN A MALE COMES ALONG WITH SUCH A TALENT FOR HUNTING THAT HE EARNS THE RIGHT TO USE THE NAME.

I AM THAT MALE. ARTEMIS THE HUNTER. I HUNTED YOU.

Below us, Jon Spiro begins to lose his mind.

WHERE DID HE GO? WHERE DID THE BOY GO?

WHERE IS HE?

I dropped down, hidden by my fairy shield. Then made Artemis "disappear" with a sheet of camo foil while I dragged him straight up to the ceiling.

Simple. But effective.

THIS ISN'T OVER, ARTEMIS FOWL.

To everyone else in the room, it seemed like he just vanished.

I WILL FIND YOU. I WILL NEVER GIVE UP! I WILL FIND YOU! YOU'VE GOT JON SPIRO'S WORD ON IT!

BDAM!

"Holly to Juliet. The principal is clear but Spiro is shooting up the lab."

"Okay, Holly, I'm going in."

"Negative. Wait for SWAT. Anyway, we want Spiro conscious."

"You take out their weapons. I'll handle the rest."

"On three."

"Juliet."

"I'm going on three."

"Okay."

I see Juliet come through the elevator doors and I unshield to fire.

Everything depends o the next few seconds.

Juliet comes through the door so fast her limbs are a blur.

My first shot takes the gun out of Pex's hands. My second does the same for Chips.

I have less than a minute to make my move.

The circumstances are hardly ideal—screaming, gunfire and general mayhem.

But then again, what better time to implement the final stage of my plan?

I work fast. I have to.

I scroll out the Plexiglas keyboard from the C Cube's base and in seconds I'm hacking into Spiro's bank accounts. All thirty-seven of them.

My third blasts the gun from Blunt's hands, but he's a real pro and he's still ready for Juliet...

YOU THINK YOU CAN TAKE ME?

A total of 2.8 billion dollars. Plenty to restore the Fowl family fortune.

I'm about to complete the transaction when something rather unfortunate happens. I remember my father.

AND WHAT ABOUT YOU, ARTY? WILL YOU MAKE THE JOURNEY WITH ME? WILL YOU TAKE YOUR CHANCE TO BE A HERO?

YES!

I hear Blunt's nose crack, effectively blinding him.

NO OFFENCE, MISS, BUT WE'RE GONNA HAVE TO CRUSH YOUR SKULL RIGHT ABOUT NOW.

SORRY, BOYS. I THINK YOU SHOULD GO TO SLEEP INSTEAD.

Do I really need billions of dollars?

"Will you take your chance to be a hero?"

I grit my teeth and, deducting a ten percent finder's fee, send the money to Amnesty International.

I'm not quite finished. There's one more good deed to be attended to.

The success of this venture depends on Foaly being too distracted to notice me hacking into his system.

I SAID GO TO SLEEP.

Juilet, you have to use exactly the words I mesmerized them to.

IF I MUST... OKAY, GENTLEMEN: BARNEY SAYS GO TO SLEEP.

Pex and Chips are snoring before they hit the ground.

I visit the LEP Perp Profiles and find the original search warrant for Mulch's dwelling.

I change the date so it's a day after the raid. Any good lawyer will have him out of prison in a heartbeat.

MULCH DIGGUMS

I haven't finished with you yet, Mulch Diggums.

Spiro is reduced to a gibbering wreck.

I'LL TALK TO YOU BACK AT BASE. YOU ARE A DANGER TO YOUR COMRADES AND YOURSELF.

YES, SIR. I DON'T KNOW WHAT CAME OVER ME.

"Okay, Juliet. Time for us to leave."

The SWAT team puts the cuffs on Spiro.

And then they lead him away.

The great Jon Spiro has never looked smaller.

DON'T FEEL YOU NEED TO RUSH. I OBVIOUSLY HAVE ALL THE TIME IN THE WORLD.

FOWL MANOR.

CHAPTER 11: **THE INVISIBLE MAN**

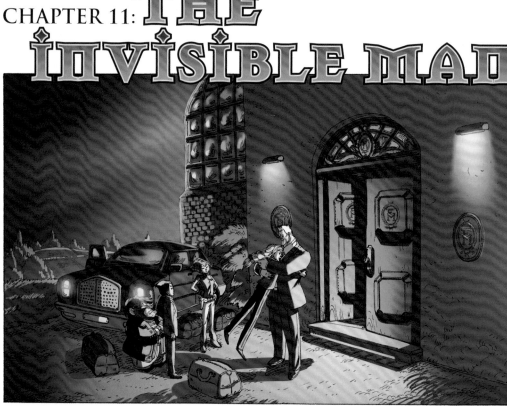

AT LEAST SHE COULD HAVE HANDCUFFED ME NEAR THE FOOD.

I THINK IF HOLLY HADN'T CAUGHT YOU IN THE AEROPLANE BATHROOM WITH A PARACHUTE, THEN SHE WOULD HAVE.

CAPTAIN SHORT, I WAS WONDERING IF I MIGHT ASK ONE LAST FAVOUR.

HOLDING CELL, HEATHROW AIRPORT, LONDON.

After the Phonetix incident, Arno Blunt escaped from custody and went on the run. He was spotted by an old contact of Butler's as he tried to pass through Customs.

Butler's eyes tell me that he thinks Blunt was heading to Ireland, looking for revenge on Artemis.

INTERVIEW PAUSED AT 2:45 P.M. NOW, DON'T GO ANYWHERE, MISTER BLUNT.

HAHA— THAT'S REAL FUNNY.

Butler doesn't want Blunt anywhere near Artemis.

THEY GOT NOTHING. NOTHING, NOTHING, NOTHING.

Same trick twice.

CONFESS.

Butler's contact gets us inside. Foaly wipes our patterns from the surveillance recordings. A sheet of camo foil does the rest.

OR I'LL SHOW YOU ROUND HELL MYSELF.

OFFICER! OFFICER! I WANNA CHANGE MY STATEMENT. I WANNA TELL YOU EVERYTHING!

I watch the LEP lugging their mind-wiping gear up the avenue, under cover of night.

If my plan doesn't work, I could be about to lose the most important memories of my life.

Butler and I have laid false trails for Foaly to follow. Undelivered emails, hidden Internet storage and a time capsule buried in the grounds.

CHAPTER 12: MIND WIPE

But if we do beat Foaly, this is how we'll do it.

MY MAN IN LIMERICK HAS FOLLOWED YOUR INSTRUCTIONS TO THE LETTER.

Three pairs of contact lenses to protect Juliet, Butler and myself from the fairy mesmer.

And this—it looks like the gold coin that Holly gave me, but it's not. It's a laser mini-disc containing every detail of the last two years.

I BRUSHED A LAYER OF GOLD LEAF ON IT. IT WON'T STAND UP TO CLOSE EXAMINATION, BUT IT'S THE BEST I COULD DO.

THANK YOU, BUTLER. THANK YOU FOR EVERYTHING.

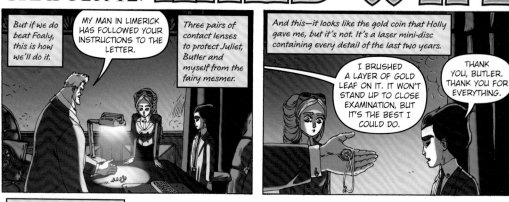

Foaly and his tech gnomes set up shop next to the maze. His equipment is incredible. He can read human minds like a book and edit out whatever he likes.

I do not like the idea of him rewriting the inside of my head.

WHAT ABOUT MY AGE? PEOPLE KNOW ME AS A FORTY-YEAR OLD MAN.

WAY AHEAD, OF YOU, BUTLER. WE HAVE A COSMETIC SURGEON WAITING TO TAKE THE YEARS OFF YOU ONCE YOU'RE ASLEEP.

YEAH, THEY INSISTED ON TAKING FAT FROM MY OWN SWEET BEHIND TO SMOOTH OUT YOUR FOREHEAD.

OH NO...FOALY, TELL ME THAT'S NOT TRUE.

IT'S KIND OF TRUE.

HEY, HAVEN'T YOU HEARD THE EXPRESSION "SMOOTH AS A DWARF'S BOTTOM"?

HEY, THERE ARE PIXIES ON THE WEST BANK PAYING A FORTUNE FOR DWARF-FAT TREATMENTS.

PLEASE MAKE SURE I DON'T REMEMBER ANY OF THIS.

HEY, IT WASN'T EXACTLY A PAIN-FREE EXTRACTION EITHER.

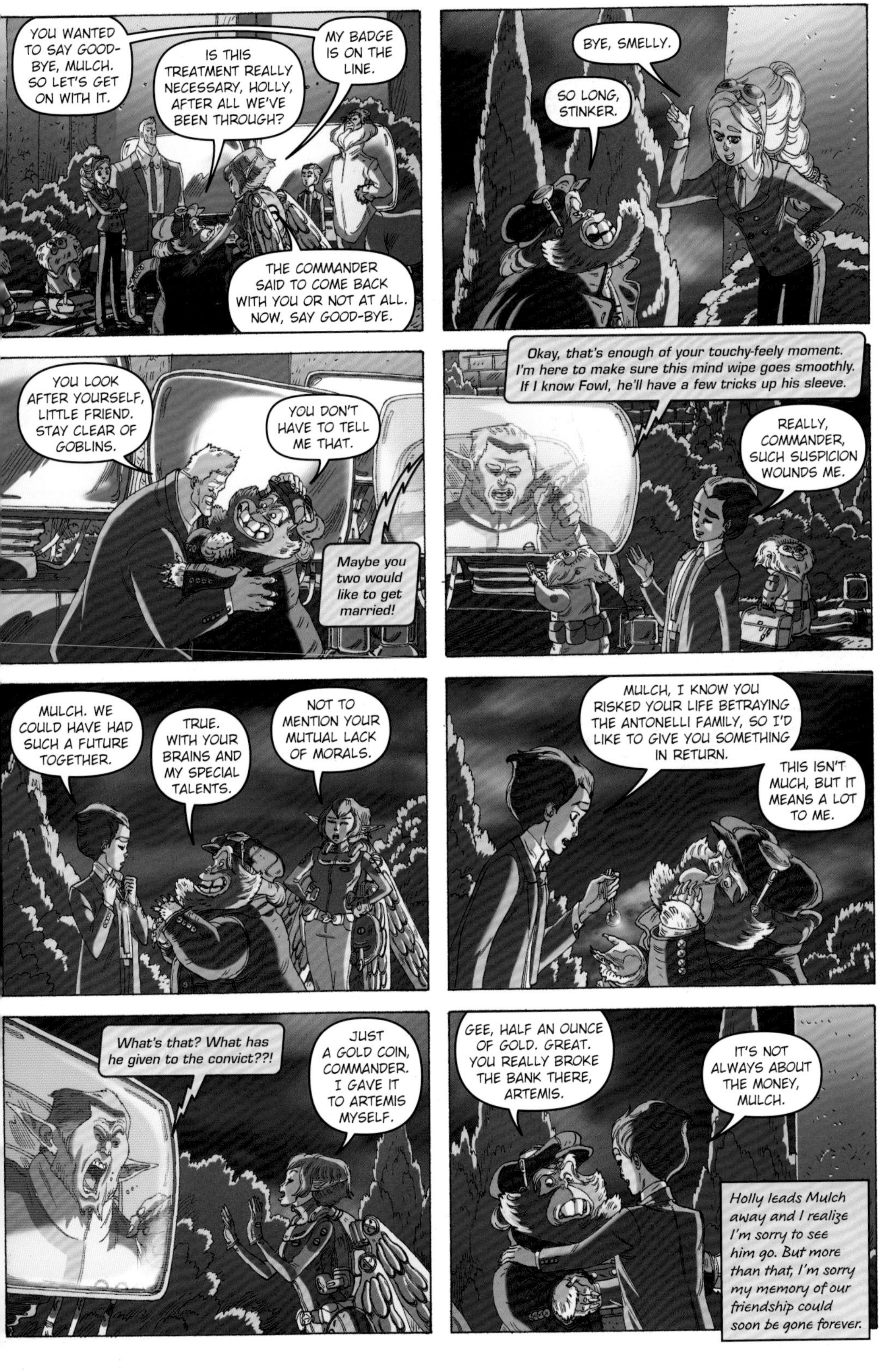
YOU WANTED TO SAY GOOD-BYE, MULCH. SO LET'S GET ON WITH IT.
IS THIS TREATMENT REALLY NECESSARY, HOLLY, AFTER ALL WE'VE BEEN THROUGH?
MY BADGE IS ON THE LINE.
THE COMMANDER SAID TO COME BACK WITH YOU OR NOT AT ALL. NOW, SAY GOOD-BYE.
BYE, SMELLY.
SO LONG, STINKER.
YOU LOOK AFTER YOURSELF, LITTLE FRIEND. STAY CLEAR OF GOBLINS.
YOU DON'T HAVE TO TELL ME THAT.
Maybe you two would like to get married!
Okay, that's enough of your touchy-feely moment. I'm here to make sure this mind wipe goes smoothly. If I know Fowl, he'll have a few tricks up his sleeve.
REALLY, COMMANDER, SUCH SUSPICION WOUNDS ME.
MULCH. WE COULD HAVE HAD SUCH A FUTURE TOGETHER.
TRUE. WITH YOUR BRAINS AND MY SPECIAL TALENTS.
NOT TO MENTION YOUR MUTUAL LACK OF MORALS.
MULCH, I KNOW YOU RISKED YOUR LIFE BETRAYING THE ANTONELLI FAMILY, SO I'D LIKE TO GIVE YOU SOMETHING IN RETURN.
THIS ISN'T MUCH, BUT IT MEANS A LOT TO ME.
What's that? What has he given to the convict??!
JUST A GOLD COIN, COMMANDER. I GAVE IT TO ARTEMIS MYSELF.
GEE, HALF AN OUNCE OF GOLD. GREAT. YOU REALLY BROKE THE BANK THERE, ARTEMIS.
IT'S NOT ALWAYS ABOUT THE MONEY, MULCH.
Holly leads Mulch away and I realize I'm sorry to see him go. But more than that, I'm sorry my memory of our friendship could soon be gone forever.

Foaly gives the signal and technicians descend like flies to a carcass.

In seconds there are electrodes attached to my temples and wrists.

NOW, ARTEMIS, I'M GOING TO MESMERIZE YOU. FOALY HAS FOUND YOUR UNDELIVERED EMAIL, AND THE ONLINE STORAGE, AND HIS TECH BOYS HAVE DUG UP YOUR TIME CAPSULE.

BUT WE HAVE TO BE SURE THERE IS NOTHING ELSE THAT MIGHT JOG YOUR MEMORY AFTER THE MIND WIPE.

IF THIS IS GOOD-BYE FOR THE LAST TIME, THEN I WANT TO SAY THANK YOU. I HAVE MY FAMILY AND FRIENDS AROUND ME, THANKS TO THE PEOPLE. I WISH I DIDN'T HAVE TO FORGET THAT.

IT'S BETTER THIS WAY, ARTEMIS, BELIEVE ME.

TELL ME, ARTEMIS, ARE THERE ANY MEMORY TRIGGERS YOU'VE HIDDEN THAT WE HAVEN'T FOUND YET? ANY AT ALL?

NO, THE TIME CAPSULE WAS OUR LAST HOPE.

Okay. The uplink is breaking up. Knock them out and wipe them.

COMMANDER, MAYBE I SHOULD ASK THE OTHERS A FEW QUESTIONS, JUST TO BE SURE?

Negative, Captain. Fowl said it himself. That was their last hope.

Hook them up and run the program.

I put the sleep masks on myself. It feels like the least I can do.

PERSONAL PROTECTION IS A COLD BUSINESS, JULIET. YOU HAVE TOO MUCH HEART FOR IT.

I'LL TRY TO HOLD ON TO THAT THOUGHT.

REMEMBER, HOLLY, IF THE PEOPLE EVER DO NEED HELP, I'M ALWAYS AVAILABLE.

I'LL REMEMBER THAT.

ARE YOU SURE ABOUT THIS, FOALY?

WHAT CHOICE DO WE HAVE? ORDERS ARE ORDERS.

"Commence Mind Wipe.

"But I'm going to keep a copy, Holly. Some time when I have a few weeks off I'm going to find out what makes Artemis Fowl tick."

There is no resistance. No struggle.

Foaly opens Artemis's synapses and he looks almost peaceful.

For once, there are no thought lines wrinkling his brow. If I didn't know him, I'd think he could almost be a normal thirteen-year-old human.

I watch as Artemis's memories are rewritten in front of my eyes.

Do the People have the right to do this?

"It's over, Holly. It's done."

BELOW GROUND.

OKAY, THEN, MASTER FOWL...

"...let's see what's so important you had to pass it to me secretly."

I have not finished with you yet, Mulch Diggums—

On your return, tell your lawyer to check the date on the original search warrant for your cave. That should get you out. When you are released keep your nose clean for a couple of years. Then bring the gold coin to me. Together we will be unstoppable.

Your friend and benefactor,
Artemis Fowl the Second

WELL, WHAT DO YOU KNOW...

"...maybe there is hope."

I have decided to keep a diary. In fact, I am surprised I haven't done so before.

Since his escape from Russia, he is full of notions of nobility and heroism.

I will need to keep such a document away from law-enforcement agencies and, for that matter, my own father.

The family fortune is in my young hands.

EPÍLOGVE I

I will continue my ingenious plots, of course.

Out of respect to my father, I will, however, change my criteria for victim selection.

I will target global corporations that the world will be better off without.

My father is not the only one to have changed.

Butler has grown older almost overnight. His appearance is the same as ever, but he has slowed down considerably.

Perhaps Juliet will step in and protect me. Although she now claims a life as a bodyguard is not for her.

Next week, she travels to the United States to try out for a professional wrestling team. I cannot help but wish her well.

But my thoughts about family issues must be suspended temporarily.

For today I discovered that I am the victim of a conspiracy.

This morning, as I washed my face at the basin, a tiny object fell from one of my eyes.

Close examination revealed it to be a corroded, tinted contact lens.

Not only that, but a mirrored layer had been added behind the tinted lens. Ingenious.

Imagine my surprise when Butler and Juliet also discovered mirrored lenses in their eyes.

Strange, but I cannot help feeling the answer is hidden somewhere in my own mind.

The lenses are clearly the work of a master craftsman and Butler is on his way to a contact, an expert in the field, who may recognize the intruder's handiwork.

Make no mistake. I will track the culprit down.

So a new chapter begins in the life of Artemis Fowl the Second.

In a matter of days my father will return home with his newfound conscience. Shortly afterwards I will be shipped off to boarding school.

Overwhelming difficulties, you may think.

But I am Artemis Fowl.

I will not be turned from my path.

I will find whoever planted those lenses and they will pay for their presumption.

And once I am rid of that nuisance, my plans will proceed unhindered.

The world will remember the name of Artemis Fowl.

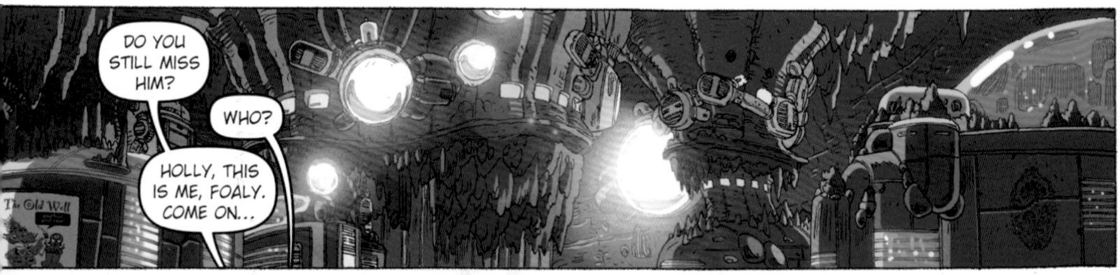
DO YOU STILL MISS HIM?
WHO?
HOLLY, THIS IS ME, FOALY. COME ON...

EPILOGUE II

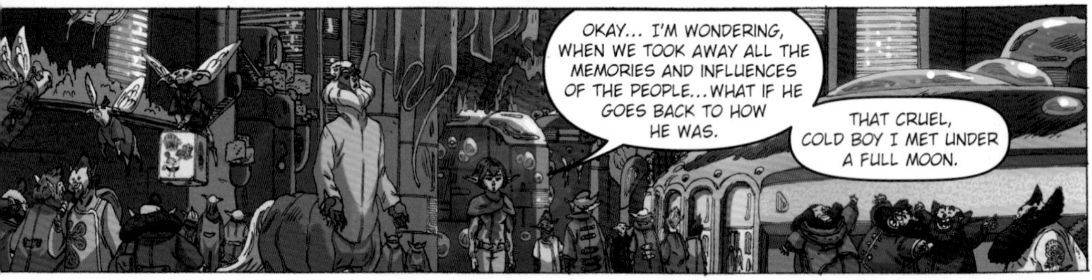
OKAY... I'M WONDERING, WHEN WE TOOK AWAY ALL THE MEMORIES AND INFLUENCES OF THE PEOPLE...WHAT IF HE GOES BACK TO HOW HE WAS.
THAT CRUEL, COLD BOY I MET UNDER A FULL MOON.

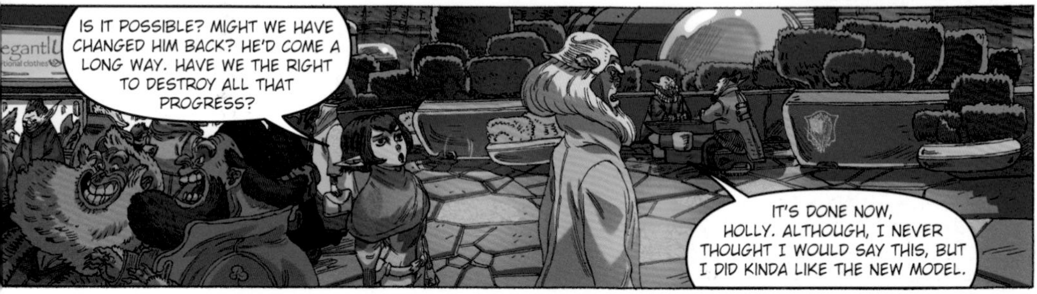
IS IT POSSIBLE? MIGHT WE HAVE CHANGED HIM BACK? HE'D COME A LONG WAY. HAVE WE THE RIGHT TO DESTROY ALL THAT PROGRESS?
IT'S DONE NOW, HOLLY. ALTHOUGH, I NEVER THOUGHT I WOULD SAY THIS, BUT I DID KINDA LIKE THE NEW MODEL.

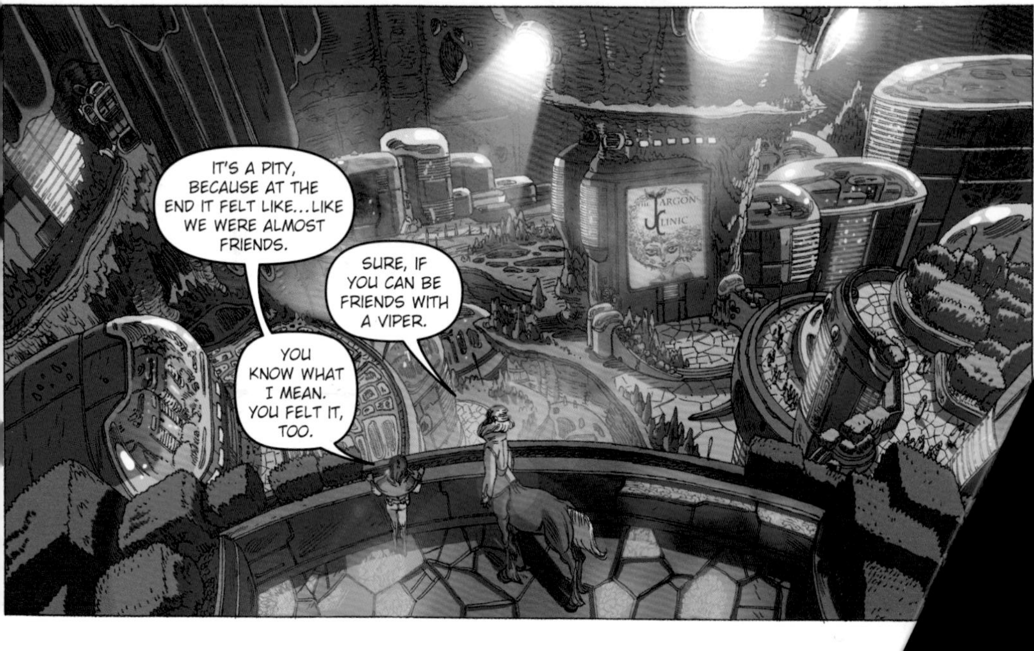
IT'S A PITY, BECAUSE AT THE END IT FELT LIKE...LIKE WE WERE ALMOST FRIENDS.
SURE, IF YOU CAN BE FRIENDS WITH A VIPER.
YOU KNOW WHAT I MEAN. YOU FELT IT, TOO.

"Well, maybe I did, Holly, and maybe I didn't. But that Artemis is gone now. Forever."

"He doesn't remember the People.

OPAL KOBOI - TOP SECURITY PATIENT
GENIUS AND MEGALOMANIAC
PUBLIC ENEMY NUMBER ONE

"Or me.

"Or even you, Holly."

"Like you said at the time, it's better that way."

BEEEEEEEEP

"After all, why would the People ever want Artemis Fowl back?"